Where Long Shadows End

More Books by Brittni Brinn

The Patch Project
A Place That Used To Be

More Books from
Adventure Worlds Press

No Light Tomorrow
The Space Between Houses

The Synthetic Albatross
Series

The Thinking Machine
The Neon Heart
Broadcast Wasteland
Break/Interrupt
Snow from a Distant Sky

Where Long Shadows End

Brittni Brinn

Where Long Shadows End
AdventureWorldsPress.com

First Printing, July 2022

Printed in Canada.

Published by
Adventure Worlds Press
Windsor, Ontario

ISBN 978-1-7776616-2-5 (Paperback)

Edited by Amilcar John Nogueira
Layout by Ben Van Dongen
Cover design by Christian Laforet

*For my grandmothers
Mary, Harriet, and Marion*

People and Locations (Spring, Year 6)

Drawn from the Phone Book records and first-person accounts from the Cabinhouse Archive. Family members share the same line; ongoing relationships are indicated by '&'.

At *Ulway's Restaurant and Retreat Centre*
Arissa, Ulway (Theodore)
May & Isak, Lucas
Rhonda & Nick
Markus & Stef
Sophie
Victoria

At the Forager Camp
Asin
Lily & Julius
Reah

In the Wasteland
Pinot
Jeff & Caden
Irene
Jax
The Survival Units

Unknown
Ed

Prologue

Isak looked around, disoriented. He was standing outside, facing a burned-up acre that spilled over a ridge above a flatline plain. The huge red sun hung heavy over the wasteland.

Had he skipped forward? Why? He tried to remember where he had just been, but came up empty. The desire was usually so strong when he jumped through time. Barely a second to blink between the wanting and the having. The curse of instant gratification.

Isak shifted his weight from his bad leg. Something snapped underfoot. Startled, he caught his balance and then froze. The broken, charred board was familiar.

"Hello?" His cry echoed, no walls or trees to contain it. Sunset tinged the burned ruins around him red.

He knew this place. He recognized the board, part of a dining table he'd sat at hundreds of times. He knew that the square-cut logs sticking up around him used to support a two-story restaurant in the middle of a vast forest. He knew that he was alone and that everyone he loved was gone.

Before all that he knew could fully register, Isak heard distant footsteps coming up behind him. "What did I want?" he racked his brain as the footsteps drew closer. "What brought me here?"

The footsteps reached him. Isak caught a glimpse of a white streak in dark hair as someone familiar passed by. They continued for a couple of steps and then stopped, their back to him. They wore a leather jacket, mud-splattered jeans, hiking boots—nothing particularly significant. Maybe it was the way they stood with their hands deep in their pockets that gave them away. In addition to all the other things he recognized about this place, Isak recognized her.

"How long has it been?" he asked.

She stared beyond the ruins of *Ulway's Restaurant and Retreat Centre*, out into the wasteland. "This is what you wanted, isn't it?" Pinot finally said, turning her ageless face towards him. "For everything to be over?"

Book One
Year 6

Chapter 1
Pinot in the Spring

16 months earlier

Pinot had delivered the message. Over the days and nights spent crossing the wasteland alone, she'd crafted the perfect phrase. Brief. To the point. Enough to cut ties with the restaurant and make sure no one came looking for her.

She delivered it standing on the creek bank, the two women on the other side tense and strange. Across the water, Arissa and May had seemed hazy, unreal.

But she'd delivered it, she was sure of that.

"When Ed gets here," she said, her throat resisting the words after days of silence, "tell him not to look for me."

She was almost back to the trees when May's voice floated over to her, fragile as a dragonfly wing. "We miss you."

We miss you.

Was that what kept Pinot from leaving, the reason she was spending the night under a tarp in the woods? Because of that one small phrase?

It was stupid, she told herself. Stupid to stay, but equally as stupid to go. She'd thought that after the message was delivered, she'd return to the empty plain, start a new life as a Grafter, and try to forget. As it turned out, it wouldn't be that easy. She had no food stores, very few supplies. Surviving on the wasteland would take much more than luck.

Pinot shifted onto her side, pulling the tarp close around her. The numbness in her core sharpened into hunger pangs. She'd filled up on water upstream from where she met May and Arissa, but her stomach hadn't been fooled for long. She needed somewhere to hole up for a few days, gather some food.

A spark of memory—May and Isak returning to the restaurant after summering at a small cabin not too far away. The cabin should be vacant. Pinot only had a vague idea of where it was, but with hunger driving her, she shot up, folded the tarp, and tucked it into her slim backpack.

The night was silver and cold, the early spring barely managing to take the edge off. Pinot's breath went up ahead of her as she navigated over tree roots, steadying herself on black tree trunks, the full moonlight scribbled over by branches. She crossed the creek where a small line of rocks emerged from the water. She faltered halfway across, one of her feet slipping into the icy water, drenching her leg up to the knee.

Ed laughed at her. She saw him clearly on the bank ahead in full colour, his messy hair burning like a red flame, his thin shoulders shaking with silent laughter. He was wearing his oversized canvas jacket and jeans, a pen and a bundle of note paper sticking out of his pocket. Exactly the way he was the morning she'd left the garage to get supplies. The way he would never be again.

Before Pinot could break the silence, Ed winked and backed into the woods.

"Wait!" Pinot splashed after him, ecstatic. Ed was okay, she thought as she mounted the opposite creek bank. He wasn't dead, he was here, waiting for her. He hadn't been taken away after all.

She came across a worn path where Ed had disappeared. Stopping to catch her breath, she peered further down the moonlit lane. It was empty.

A flapping sound came from overhead. Pinot spotted a bit of red tape tied around a birch tree, the ends lifting in the breeze.

Red. Ed's apparition. A trick of the night.

Pinot gripped the pen lid deep in her pocket.

The worn path led to the cabin. The door and windows were boarded up, a line of red tape strung across the porch entrance. Pinot made her way around the back, trailing a hand along the rough exterior wall. The back door was barred, a single board nailed across the frame.

Pinot ignored the board, ducking down to study the handle. It was a simple lock mechanism, no deadbolt. She straightened up and with every bit of strength she had left brought her boot down on the doorknob. It shifted but held. She pummelled the door around it with a series of kicks until the old wood gave way and buckled under her barrage.

With one last kick, the door banged free. Pinot breathed heavily, holding her stomach and waiting for something to come barreling out at her from the shadowed interior. Nothing happened.

She entered the cabin, her senses sharpened by adrenaline. Kitchen table, couch, a stack of logs in the corner next to a cast-iron fireplace. Other than that, it was empty.

Pinot shut the door behind her, sliding the table against it. She scoured the cupboards and found one can of soup, but nothing to open it with. With a roar of frustration, she threw it to the floor. The can rolled under the table, unharmed.

Hungry, exhausted, and hopeless, Pinot curled up on the couch and waited for morning to arrive.

Brittni Brinn

Chapter 2
Isak in the Spring

It was usually dark when Isak travelled through time. Barely a blink before he arrived at his destination. If he desired something strongly enough, and if that desire was fulfilled sometime in the future, he'd be pulled there. Not too far. He'd never travelled more than a few weeks ahead, and over the past couple of years his powers had diminished.

When Isak reached for Lucas, who was about to fall from the dining hall table, he suddenly yearned for a quiet place to talk with May. He missed the cabin where they used to live, just the two of them with their little boy. Arissa and the rest of the restaurant crowd were good people, but there was never any true, honest-to-god privacy. He had no idea how May had been feeling lately, and he desperately wanted to.

Before he could dilute the desire, push it back to a lukewarm idea, he felt the pull of the future thrill through him.

Not now! He rushed to lift Lucas safely back onto the table. Isak blinked.

The dining hall twisted around him. He stood still as ethereal images and ghostly figures converged around him. Whirring lights and laughter, smells of lightning ozone, the forest crackling beneath him as cars roared overhead.

Frozen, Isak held Lucas in front of him. The baby stared at him with trusting eyes, the bronze starburst in each brown iris glowing from within. Lucas's eyes were the only constant in the surreal rush of time around them. As Isak watched, his baby matured into a child, then an adult, his hair going grey and his cheeks caving in. Horrified, Isak tried to release his hold, but his hands remained fixed around Lucas as his elderly child ripened into adulthood, morphed into adolescence, compacted into childhood, then relaxed once again into infancy.

Time untwisted, and the ghostly lights and figures disappeared.

Lucas's soft cry brought Isak into the new present. They had both skipped ahead to a quiet place in the woods outside of the restaurant. The sun was coming up over the trees, casting long morning shadows.

Isak's breath went up in a cloud. He found he could move. Resting Lucas against his chest, he slowly sank onto the log bench behind him. He watched the clouds drift over the forest as he drew cold air into his lungs and moved it outwards.

This was his and May's bench, he realised. They'd made it in the fall, before the snow swallowed it up. If there was a private place at the restaurant for them to talk, this was it.

Isak heard her come up behind him. As May lifted Lucas away, Isak knew exactly what she was thinking and felt ashamed. He waited in silence, but the feeling was all that she gave him. He understood. Her footsteps faded; the distant echo of the restaurant's heavy front door closing came to him like an afterthought.

Isak sat there for a long time. The phantasms of light roiled through his mind. He had never seen anything during his trips through time before. At best, he had impressions, an eye or hand, but he always believed that it was God's guidance moving him like a chess piece across the board of time. Not these nightmarish visions, not Lucas ageing and youthening before him, his own frozen hands expanding around the child.

For the first time, Isak felt the true horror of his ability. The ill-nature of it. It was a crime against nature to waste the only thing he had as a human being: the concept and passage of time.

Who was he, to jump over that gift, with all its hurts and happiness, to demand his own will and skip whatever lessons time had to teach him?

But he couldn't stop it. He could only turn the future aside when the desire rose in him. Enslaved by passion, as philosophers said, unable to live in a world of logic alone. Was that his fault, being a human, a mind and body, an animal and soul bound together? His ability made him recognize the material side of him, that wild part within him that wanted. He could never divide himself fully from that, especially since the things he wanted were things he needed to survive: food, water, beauty, love. The short reach of his ability contained him to small things, small moments he yearned for. It wasn't wrong to want those things. It was nature.

Only the Event had twisted his nature. And now, it was affecting Lucas.

Did he really bring Lucas with him into that incomprehensible middle space? That was something he hadn't intended, not wanted at all. Was it because he was holding Lucas the moment he jumped? No—Isak had skipped forward while in contact with May before and she'd never come with him. She lived through time in its usual flow, could tell him how long he'd been away. So if it wasn't his ability that brought Lucas forward, could it be that his son had inherited some of his power?

Jumping up from the bench, Isak hurried as best as he could through the forest behind the restaurant. Passing by the small row of carved stones where Milo had been buried during the winter, he went through the newly-planted gardens, covered with tarps to protect against spring frosts. Isak followed the red dirt path that ran beside the log wall. He came to the front door, the faded *Ulway's Restaurant and Retreat Centre* sign barely holding onto the crossbar it was nailed to. Isak passed under it as he rubbed his numb hands together.

Would Lucas be alright? The thought struck deep. What if the trip had been too much for him? Isak hadn't thought to check. It had been enough in the moment to feel the warm living bundle of a human settle into his arms.

"May?" Isak shouted into the dining area. Stef and Markus looked up from their conversation across the room.

"You're back." Arissa pushed through the door to the kitchen and let it swing shut behind her. Her tightly-curled black and grey hair flared around her face as she came up to him. There was something in her expression that made him feel uneasy. "Where is Lucas?"

"May has him," Isak explained. "He's alright."

Across the room, Stef and Marcus pointed towards the stairs.

"Thank God," Arissa breathed. Without another word, she turned away from him and went downstairs. Isak heard her knock on the door to his and May's room, and the dim creak of the door as it opened and shut below.

Isak felt Stef and Markus's eyes on him. He didn't want to follow Arissa now, not when she was clearly on May's side. Instead, he found himself drifting down the hallway to the clinic.

The door was unlocked. Isak settled on the padded bench inside and pulled an icon of Mary, one he had worn since childhood, from inside his shirt and held it tight in his hand. The narrow window over the counter cast grey light over the jars below, filled with gauze and tweezers and other medical supplies.

After a while, Isak kissed the icon and tucked it back into his shirt. He took a deep breath and let it out slowly. He hadn't been to the clinic for a while. Pinot's clinic. After she left, Arissa had taken over caring for sick residents—luckily, the winter had been kind to him.

Isak wondered where Pinot had been all this time. She and Ed had gone off the previous fall after Pinot disembowelled a dangerous Grafter, saving May and Lucas in the process. Before the rescue, May had resented Pinot for offering to abort May's pregnancy. Once she was gone, May had softened her attitude, almost returning to a state of benevolence towards Pinot's memory. But that benevolence came with shame as well—after all, May had instigated the plan that caused Jax to leave the restaurant and, by extension, Pinot's broken heart.

Isak usually didn't bring up anything to do with Pinot, knowing how it affected May. But here in the place where Pinot had spent her time helping others, he was free to think about her with gratitude and regret. Maybe if he'd been more supportive, Pinot wouldn't have resorted to violence and run away.

He turned aside the wish to see her again, fearing another leap through time. It was May he should go see now, see what the damage was. He sighed, knowing that he shouldn't be hiding in this grey room, heavy with the past. The past, however, was safe. He could never go back there again.

He met Arissa on the stairs. As they passed, she gave him a small nod. He continued down, his heart sinking. Whatever the nod meant, it had not been encouraging.

With a soft knock, Isak went into the small room he shared with his family. May waited in front of the crib, standing between him and Lucas.

"I don't want you near him." May crossed her arms. "Not until we know what's going on."

Isak sat on the bed, rubbing his leg. The morning cold had stiffened his old injury, probed into it. After a moment, he nodded. "That's probably best."

"It was different before," May continued. "I thought if you skipped ahead while holding him, Lucas would fall, or get hurt. But now…" She let out a shuddering breath. "Time travel? How will it affect him? Is it something he can do alone, or does he need to be in contact with you? There are too many things that could go wrong. I will not lose him, understand?"

The accusation in her voice stung. "I don't want anything to happen to him either. And I didn't want to bring him with me. I didn't want this to happen!"

May sat next to him on the bed. After a moment, she reached over and took his hand. "Promise me it won't happen again."

Isak ripped his hand away and scanned her pale face. "You're not...changing my feelings, are you?"

May stood up. "I'm not using my powers on you, if that's what you're asking!"

"Are you, May?"

"I stopped doing that after...after what happened with Jax." She went over to Lucas's crib, her back to Isak. "I'm not trying to control you." Her voice was strained. "But this is important. We have to be on the same page about this."

"We are," Isak replied. He stood up from the bed and gathered a few of his clothes from the dresser. Then, he made the long walk to the bedroom door, closing it gently behind him.

Chapter 3
Rhonda Makes Films

Most days, Rhonda had to make films in her head. When her camera battery ran out of juice, she couldn't just plug it in for a recharge. The gasoline-powered generator in the kitchen was the only power source left at the restaurant and if too many things ran at once, the machine complained. Since Ed's departure the previous fall, the computers in the dining hall had been dismantled. Power usage was tightly scheduled. Rhonda only had access to short bursts of power when the generator was unused.

Even without her camera, Rhonda couldn't help reframing the world around her: the scene of wind-blown clouds overhead, a rabbit crossing the road outside the restaurant, Stef and Markus talking in low voices at a dining hall table. Little moments that Rhonda let imprint on her retinas and project into her mind.

She'd tried to find other ways of letting the images out—writing them down on scraps of paper or sketching them with pencil stubs on the wall near her bed. But she'd stopped that early on. She wasn't a good artist and it was embarrassing to have people stop on their way through the dorm to peer at her outlines scribbled on the drywall.

What else could she do? Nothing else satiated her need to link moving visions, add music, fill the gaps with b-roll, and cut artistically between one image and the next. A melange of people and places and things crowded her mind, vying for attention:

The coffee cup set on the windowsill, fog-swathed trees looming outside of it—

Sunlight on the snow blanketing the garden plots they would plant in the spring—

The stark contrast of light and shadow on someone's arm—usually Nick's.

Nick eating dry cereal in the morning, Nick with sweat on his face, Nick's glossy blond hair tickling her face. The close-up moments, the dim light in the storage room masking his expression, only their heavy breathing and suppressed moans to fill the scene. Nick stretching in the woods, not realising that she waited behind him, admiring his resolve to go out running every day—who does that? In the apocalypse, especially.

She would call her film *Apocalypse Now*—wait, that was taken already, wasn't it? Or did it even count, if it had been destroyed with the world, erased? Her preference for originality made her cycle through other options: *All the Apocalypses of Yesterday, All I Got from the Apocalypse Was This Lousy Party Favour, Apocalypse…* didn't have to be part of the title. Because that was the thing about an apocalypse—it didn't *stay* the apocalypse, did it?

Almost six years after the Event, she wasn't living in the apocalypse anymore: this was something new, for better or worse. After the apocalypse, that turning point where everything changed, the world kept going.

It was something important, Rhonda thought, realising the world was not made for you. Humankind could throw a tantrum, like Lucas hitting the floor with his tiny fists, but the world would go on in its own way, its own time. Even if the world was destroyed, the universe would keep going. Even if the universe perished in a terrible heat death, something would go on. The end, the apocalypse, was always the start of something else.

Rhonda connected her camera to the computer tower she'd moved to a little-used desk in the corner of the kitchen. She had to charge the battery though the computer, since the generator only had three-prong inputs. While it charged, she turned on the attached monitor and drifted through the computer's files, revisiting old board messages, playing a level on Ed's defunct video game, and reviewing her films.

She watched a bit she'd filmed before she came to *Ulway's*. Milo was in the garden behind the school where they used to live, tying a sunflower to a trellis. It was already taller than him, and as he tied it, the yellow petals brushed his white hair. Noticing her behind him, he turned slightly and smiled without showing his teeth, crow's feet deepening into his wrinkled skin. Then, the camera cut away.

She watched it a few times, still feeling the aftershocks of his death a few months before. Even though she went to his grave almost every day, she sometimes forgot that he was gone.

She'd tucked his watch away in her backpack under her bed with her old USB drive. It felt wrong to wear it: she'd been angry with him the last time they spoke. If she put it on now, his spirit would know—the watch would draw him back, and he would place a hand on her shoulder and smile, forgiving her.

Rhonda didn't want that. She wanted his spirit to rest with his wife and his daughter. After all, Rhonda wasn't his real family. They'd survived the Event together by chance, a student and a janitor in a little-used corner of a university.

Circumstances had made them family. She had every right to wear the watch he'd left her. But it was still too fresh, his illness. His death.

She didn't talk to Nick about her feelings. Nick had been serious and comforting for the first few weeks, carefully tending to her grief. When he thought she'd recovered, Nick returned to the open and carefree person she'd fallen in love with. But she felt a rawness, a loneliness, whenever she lingered too long on Milo's death, like she was standing alone in the middle of the wasteland.

Maybe if Pinot had been there…but no. Pinot abandoned Milo and all the other residents. Even though Pinot had been clear from the start that she couldn't heal Milo's cancer, she could've done more to ease his suffering. Pinot didn't care. She'd gone away, and didn't bother coming back. Maybe she was dead.

Rhonda grimaced. She didn't want that, did she? Pinot, dead? Death was horrible. The end of an embodied life. No more chances. No more joy. She didn't wish that on anyone.

The battery indicator on the camera beeped, signalling a full charge. She shut down the computer and bundled the camera and the charging cable into her bag. The battery would last about eight hours. She'd have to unload the footage onto the computer sometime mid-week—hopefully, Sophie would allow her an extra spot on the generator schedule. It was frustrating to always be behind on filming the things she imagined. But something was better than nothing, she told herself. It was better than nothing.

Log Entry 0:

In case someone finds this Survival Unit—

Prop the hatch open. Wedge it open however you can and make sure it cannot be sealed. Otherwise, you may be trapped inside—as we were. Do it, <u>right now.</u>

Now, open the main file on the right-hand screen. Inside are instructions on how to access the wealth of scientific data stored in this S.U., from before the Event to the present day. My present day, anyway.

And you'll find logs. About the weapon. About the threat. In case I couldn't stop it.

Look over your shoulder. Make sure the hatch is still open.

If the siren sounds, <u>GET OUT</u>.

Chapter 4
Isak and the Cabin

There were three communal sleeping rooms to choose from. Standing at the bottom of the stairs, Isak picked the one on the right. Six cot-like beds were set around the room at random, some flanked by nightstands or stacks of storage bins to create a sense of privacy. It was around 8:00 pm, way before when he usually slept, but Isak was exhausted from avoiding May all day.

Sophie was the only person already in bed, her grey hair in braids under her nightcap, the grey blanket pulled tight to her chin. She sat up slowly when Isak came in.

"So it's like that," she said, looking at him with pity. "It's such a shame."

"I'm fine." Isak picked a bare cot next to the window and unfolded a set of grey sheets over it.

Sophie grunted, as if thinking of something, but Isak pretended not to hear. He got under the wool blanket without changing out of his clothes and settled as well as he could on the thin mattress.

"Goodnight," Sophie said. The springs on her cot squeaked as she turned over.

Evening faded to twilight. Moonlight filtered in through Isak's window. A few stars hung above the solid black trees. He relaxed a little. His room with May didn't have any windows. If there was a silver lining to sleeping alone, it was the clear view of the night sky. He knew that in the morning, the separation would hurt, but for now, he embraced oblivion and prayed for relief.

***

When they met at breakfast the next morning, May was polite but distant. Isak quickly kissed Lucas on the forehead and went about scooping a small portion of hashbrowns and eggs onto a cracked plate. He took a step toward the tables in the dining hall then stopped. Would May sit with him? He held his plate steady and took a deep breath.

"Hey, Isak!" Nick said from one of the tables. The younger man waved him over.

Isak settled into a chair across from him. "I'm fine," Isak answered the unspoken sympathy. He watched as May picked up a few things from the breakfast table and carried Lucas back downstairs.

"...but Lucas is okay, right?" Nick asked once May had disappeared.

"As far as I know." Isak swallowed a forkful of eggs through a rush of guilt. Had he really not checked Lucas more closely after bringing him through time?

"I'm sure it'll blow over," Nick said about the apparently well-known fact that Isak and May had slept in separate rooms. "May'll see. No harm, no foul, yeah? Not like you meant to take Lucas with you."

"That's what I told her," Isak replied without much enthusiasm. He pushed a hunk of hashbrown across his plate.

Nick, however, had enough enthusiasm for the two of them. "Come on!" Nick jumped up, shaking dry cereal crumbs from his light jacket and sweatpants. "I wanna show you something." He turned and jogged, his running shoes squeaking as they moved from carpet to the linoleum strip leading to the front entranceway.

Caught in Nick's rush, Isak got up to join him. He groaned as his old leg injury seized up. In fact, his whole body felt tight from the uncomfortable night on the cot. Maybe he should stay

24

here, stack up a couple more thin mattresses, and sleep all day.

Nick popped his head back into the dining hall. "Isak!" he yelled.

Sighing, Isak stretched his leg behind him. The tightness eased. Leaving his breakfast, Isak followed Nick out of the restaurant.

It was warmer outside than it had been the previous morning. The sky was a saturated blue. Somewhere down the ridge, a woodpecker tapped a greeting.

"Wait up!" Isak called after Nick, who had started off down the front road.

Nick turned, jogging on the spot.

"I can't keep up with you if you're going to run."

"No problem," Nick beamed, his feet slowing to a soft patter on the gravel. "I'll match pace with you."

They crossed the creek and veered north. Isak recognized the pine needle-scattered pathway, the bright red strips of tape tied around the occasional tree.

"Why are we—?" Isak started to ask.

Nick held up a hand, pressing a finger to his mouth.

Familiar with the path, Isak easily followed him for the last few metres. He was confused, however, when Nick pulled him down to a crouch behind a tree trunk covered in water-speckled moss. At the end of the path was the cabin. The doors and windows were boarded over—exactly the way Isak and May had left it the previous fall.

"Someone's been using it." Nick pointed to a scattering of fish bones along the path and the new tarp secured over part of a boarded-up window.

"Have you seen them?" Isak replied, easing his weight off his bad leg. The idea of someone staying where he'd lived not too long ago felt strange. Unsettling.

Nick shook his head. "I run by here sometimes. Just started noticing little things."

"Think it's a Grafter?" Isak whispered, his hand pressing the icon under his shirt. The dangerous scavengers sometimes ventured in from the wasteland, looking for food and supplies. During the time Isak had been at *Ulway's*, only a few Grafters had made it up to the restaurant. The last one had held the place hostage; it was only thanks to Pinot and Ed's quick thinking that no one had been hurt. Apart from the Grafter, that was.

"Should we take a closer look?" Nick grinned.

"What? They could be dangerous!"

"I thought we could look in, let Arissa know what we find. If it gets dicey, you can skip ahead, right? I'll run. We'll be fine."

"Okay," Isak agreed, curious in spite of himself. It was strange to be crouching outside the cabin that he'd missed just the day before. If only he and May had gone back for the spring, maybe May would've trusted him with Lucas.

"There's a window on the left side," Isak told Nick. "It's higher than the other ones. May and I never bothered to board it up. If you give me a boost, I'll get a full view."

"Alright!" Nick cheered in a whisper. "Let's do it."

They snuck around to the side of the cabin. Nick braced his back against the rough wood wall, offering his laced hands for Isak to step into.

Not as tall as Nick and not nearly in as good of shape, Isak stumbled a little getting up in the makeshift foothold, but together they managed.

"This feels like being a kid at summer camp," Isak mused. He remembered standing on another boy's shoulders to spy on counsellor meetings just for the thrill of observing while remaining unseen.

On level with the high window, Isak wiped some grime from the pane and looked inside. The dim interior of the cabin resolved into a familiar floor plan: a rough square split between a kitchen, a fireplace, and the pull-out couch at the centre of the room. The bird's eye view gave Isak a new appreciation for how compact the space was. He could see the whole of it without having to turn his head.

New details came into focus. Dishes on the table, clothes and tarps along the floor. A pile of blankets on the couch. Not only blankets. The gleam of someone's eyes within, watching him.

Isak gasped and dropped down.

"Hey!" Nick exclaimed, thrown off-balance.

"They saw me!"

"Let's go!" Nick ran.

Caught in the moment, Isak took off after him.

They stopped where the path rejoined the creek. Isak braced a hand on his good knee, gasping for breath.

Nick stood and listened, his chest rising slightly as he scanned the woods behind them. He gave Isak an encouraging pat on the back and led the way up through the trees.

Isak settled on a brisk pace as he crested the main road to the restaurant. His leg ached, but the rest of his body felt a lot better after the time outside.

They found Arissa at work in the garden and told her about the stranger in the cabin.

"I'll send Stef and Markus to check it out," she said, clearing some brush from the vegetable plot. "It could just be a traveller on their way through."

Twenty minutes later, Stef and Markus returned from their survey. They reported that the cabin had been hurriedly vacated, the back door left wide open.

"Looks like you scared them off," Stef elbowed Nick in the ribs. "Shoulda come to us in the first place. We run the security around here, after all."

"I thought it'd be fun," Nick gave her a friendly punch on the shoulder and winked at Markus. "Besides, Isak needed something to take his mind off things."

Isak felt a warm rush of gratitude. The adventure had definitely distracted him from his argument with May. "But who was inside?" he said.

"We'll probably never know," Arissa sighed. "Would you two mind taking an extra patrol shift tonight, just in case?"

Nick threw an arm over Isak's shoulders. "We'd be delighted."

Chapter 5
Pinot in the Woods

Pinot jumped up from the couch where she'd dozed off. The face in the window dropped away. She heard voices and movement in the brush outside the cabin. Someone had seen her. She hadn't been careful enough.

When the sounds outside faded, Pinot got to work. She packed up her clothes, a tarp, and a blanket. Someone would be back. Either a search party from *Ulway's* or a Grafter looking for easy supplies. Pinot thought the face in the window had been Isak's—the tan skin and shoulder-length black hair—but she hadn't seen enough to be sure. She didn't want Arissa to know she was still in the area after she'd delivered her message and severed her ties. If it was a Grafter, she couldn't take any chances.

Pinot paused, scanning the room with regret. She'd sheltered here just over a week, living off morel mushrooms, fiddleheads, and tiny fish from the stream. She'd put on a bit of weight. Her joints no longer ached, and she felt alert and well-rested for the first time that she could remember. Her trip back through the wasteland had left her a wraith—emaciated, passionless, drifting through pain and hunger and terror without much response. At least then, there had been no grief. No guilt.

Shouldering the full bag, Pinot left by the back door and finding no one outside, hiked into the woods.

During her first night, Pinot caught a rabbit in a makeshift snare and killed it with a sharpened rock. She used the same rock to skin it, her hands getting cut and bloody as she seperated skin from flesh, fat from bone. She got a fire going with her old lighter and some dead pine branches. She skewered the rabbit meat on a stick, half of it burning as it hung into the flames. Ravenous, she didn't care. As she lifted the charred meat to her mouth, she paused, overwhelmed by a rush of gratitude. Not to a god, not to the rabbit, though both were encompassed in the overflow of gratefulness for food, for being alive. Simple things. Holy things. She ate her way through the whole rabbit with tears in her eyes.

After that, the gratitude came and went. At times, it completely disappeared when it rained or her tarp ripped or she wrenched her ankle on a root. The spring was long and the nights were cold. But no matter how bad things got, Pinot did not return to *Ulway's*.

***

Living in the woods was a lot harder than Pinot had anticipated. On the wasteland, things were clear-cut: you either had water or you didn't. The figure on the horizon was either a blood-thirsty Grafter or they weren't. But the way of life in the trees was more nuanced. The animals were cheeky and dangerous all at once; a plant kept all of its toxins in one place, its fruit in another, and some parts of it existed all on their own outside of human need or interest. What a change it was from the bleak and flat lands Pinot had lived through.

She camped in the green buffer zone between the wasteland and *Ulway's*, moving locations each night. She learned to live in the lush silences of the forest, where something was always happening past the screens of leaves, under the branches strewn across the ground. She got to know where birds nested, their calls and routines. Using what little knowledge of plants she'd picked up at *Ulway's*, she determined which berries and mushrooms to avoid and how to identify stinging nettle and poison ivy. The creek was never far in this part of the woods, and she came to it daily as if to a cherished friend.

A bear lived deeper in the forest. Pinot occasionally came across tracks and had once seen it down the creek, its underbelly shaggy and dripping water. The bulk of it, the sheer presence of its size was breathtaking. An awe-inspiring giant. She'd crept backwards, holding her breath. After that, Pinot and the bear kept out of each other's way in a season-long dance, turning aside when too many signs of the other appeared.

Pinot's diet was better than it had been in a long time. She caught rabbits in snares, killing them with a sharpened piece of thin copper pipe she'd found discarded in the woods. As the spring bled into summer, Pinot became a bonafide predator. She felt a grim satisfaction that her knowledge of violence, her experience of it as a teenager, now had application.

Grafters sometimes crossed the line between the wasteland and the forest. If the Grafters were merely cutting firewood or were regulars, Pinot let them pass. If they were heading towards the restaurant with bloody intentions, Pinot dealt with them. No one would threaten the people up there again. Not if she could help it.

And during the long, dark nights wrapped in her tarp, sometimes with a fire to keep her company, she'd think about Ed.

She gave up too easily after he went missing. She'd never found a body, and there were definitely people responsible for his disappearance. But the trail had gone cold after about a day, and she'd had no choice but to return to the restaurant, to pass on a message for Ed to stay there, a place of safety, of community. A place she was no longer part of.

Back then, she'd figured that Ed would somehow get away and make it back to *Ulway's*. But her reasoning left room for regret. What if Ed couldn't escape? Where would she look for him now, where would she even start? The wasteland was huge, impossible to search on her own. She could send messages to other camps through the trading caravans, but replies would take months. She mulled over her options, but couldn't find anything satisfying.

Days passed, then weeks. The forest became all that there was. The forest and the guilt.

Chapter 6
Rhonda After the Apocalypse

Rhonda checked her bangs in the mirror. The ends were long and brushed against her eyelashes. She took the pair of scissors from the cabinet, gave them a rinse, and trimmed the too-long pieces. She'd only had bangs for a couple months, and was still getting the hang of how much to cut. She fluffed her hair and let the bangs settle naturally against her forehead. They were uneven, and there were definitely longer pieces on the left side, but it would do. Hair grew back, and in a couple days the imperfections would work themselves out.

On her way out of the bathroom, she crashed into Victoria, the restaurant's resident engineer. They both steadied themselves, Victoria with a laugh and Rhonda with a self-consciousness grunt.

Victoria noticed Rhonda's attempt at trimming her bangs. "Looking good!" she cheered.

"Thanks," Rhonda mumbled, admiring Victoria's perfectly-executed ponytail. Victoria never had the halo of loose hairs that Rhonda did when she pulled her hair back. Even when Victoria was elbow-deep into fixing the generator, oil and grease streaking her wheat-gold arms, she was more like Athena in the heat of battle than a grubby mechanic.

Rhonda's bangs shed small bits of cut hair onto her nose. Victoria went into the bathroom. Rhonda sneezed.

"Bless you!" Sophie said from the shared sleeping area across the hall. She was folding a pile of sheets that had just come off the drying line.

Rhonda nodded to her and continued through the hallway of doors to sleeping areas, bathrooms, storage closets, sitting spaces. Living at the restaurant meant that there was always someone around to bless your sneezes. Every little moment, someone around the corner, hanging out in a doorway, playing cards or making meals. It took a lot of getting used to when she and Milo had arrived. Five years with only Milo for company had definitely made her prefer calm, quiet spaces. The restaurant was exciting though, even after living there for a year. It made her feel alive, and that was something she never took for granted. Not anymore.

***

"What are you looking at?" Nick asked quietly, not wanting to startle her. But he didn't have to bother; she'd heard him coming through the woods, knew the rhythm of his walk better than anyone.

Rhonda stopped recording and returned the camera to her bag. "Just some patterns on the forest floor that looked cool." Sunlight filtered through the leaves and hit the ground with shifting ovals of light, highlighting tiny stones, ferns, moss, snails, ants, leaves, dirt, sticks, berries, droppings, bones, pine needles, raspberries, thorns, hair, fur, and footprints. She liked that about filming: the longer you looked at a scene, the more you saw. Film drew attention to things, bringing the small details into focus, forever. Well, as long as the file lasted, or the tape, or whatever. How many films had been lost during the Event? Those small moments that would never be seen again. Only remembered, played on the inner screen of recall, changing with the viewer's mood, small variations on the original vision. That was the nature of visions. They were temporary, only existed to motivate someone to action. If the vision faded, the actions would still remain. So then why waste her time on the vision, and not the action?

She couldn't help herself.

Nick settled down next to her, balancing on the soles of his shoes. His jogging pants were crisp and clean. Rhonda's jeans were smeared with moss and dirt from trying to find the right angle. She appreciated the difference. That they were so different was part of her attraction to Nick. While he was athletic and happy, she was sedentary and reserved. His blond hair was always perfect and he was undoubtedly attractive but apart from her height, Rhonda was not a person who would stand out in a crowd. She wore toques and a windbreaker and jeans, nothing special. But she liked to think that whereas Nick's style screamed yoga enthusiast, her understated clothing gave her a creative vibe. But who cared really, in the apocalypse? She smiled to herself. Of course everyone cared as much as before. The apocalypse was over, and life went on.

"I was trying to convince some folks to go mushroom hunting," Nick said, tracing a finger up her arm. He was always trying to start outdoor things—even in the dead of winter, he'd convinced Stef and Markus to build a snowman with him. Though Arissa was hesitant to let large groups leave the immediate area, she acknowledged that people got restless with the same set of walls around them all the time.

There were more safety protocols in place after the Grafter incident the previous fall. Always two people walking the perimeter, a person watching the front entrance in case someone tried to get in unnoticed. It wasn't much, but it had saved them some trouble over the winter. It gave Arissa time to meet approaching visitors outside of the building and make trade arrangements in a non-threatening way. But no one had come through the woods for the past month or so, apart from the usual trade caravan from down south.

The caravan had left a couple of people behind, which was unusual. Most people had settled into their camps, whether in Summerland out west or with the trade caravans or the various Grafter factions on the wasteland. Still, people wanting a change of scene wasn't hard to believe. Not that long ago, Rhonda herself had considered leaving the restaurant behind.

Nick nudged Rhonda. "Coming?"

"Okay," she replied, her mind still on the sunlight weaving spots along the forest floor. Nick gave her a hand up. She didn't register her surroundings again until Nick rested her against the back wall of the restaurant underneath the fire escape stairs. She welcomed his cool hands under her windbreaker, his warm lips on her neck.

"Your bangs look nice," he said, his voice husky in her ear.

"Yeah?" Her hands went into his hair as he moved to kiss her face. She returned the kiss, pushing aside her misgivings— after all, it was full daylight, and someone coming around back could easily see them. Rhonda looked out over Nick's shoulder as she undid the tie on his sweatpants. Only leaves and birds and bright spots of sunlight greeted her.

Chapter 7
Ulway's Secret

New people! Ulway thought happily. And nice people, it seemed like. The trading caravan had left them behind, one with long greying hair, the other in her late teens with close-cropped sandy brown hair. Her name was Ksenia, and her mom's name was Catherine.

"Are they staying forever?" Ulway asked his aunt.

Arissa smiled and said, "We'll see."

It took Ulway weeks to gather up his courage to approach Ksenia. He practised saying things in a mirror, but the couple of times she walked his way, he pretended to be going somewhere else. The time wasn't right! He wasn't wearing his lucky socks! He couldn't remember what he was going to say!

One morning, he went up to the bathroom mirror and gave himself a stern talking to. "Now listen, Ulway. You have to talk to her. She's nice, and you want to be her friend, so just go and do it!" Pleased with himself, he resolved to go through with it even though his palms were sweating and one of his lucky socks had a hole in the toe.

Ksenia was sitting at one of the dining tables, her freckled hands working through a mass of colourful embroidery floss.

"Hi," her gaze rose as Ulway joined her then flicked back down to her task.

"What, what are you doing?" Ulway asked. Her clear blue

eyes, freckles, and big-toothed smile were doing something weird to his insides.

She lifted her hands slightly, revealing a knotted band of colour. Each finger was wrapped in a thread, holding them apart, a rainbow in stasis. "Making a friendship bracelet."

"You can MAKE those?" Ulway asked, suddenly feeling silly. Of course, friendship bracelets, any bracelet, had to be made by somebody. He'd just never seen it done before. That Ksenia could make colourful bands of decorative knots from a tangled pile of thread raised his attraction to her to adoration.

"See?" Ksenia wove the rainbow between her fingers a couple of times, but Ulway was too enraptured with her to really take in what she was doing. "Easy," she smiled, a little embarrassed by the attention. But she kept at it as Ulway looked on in admiring silence.

"How old are you anyway?" Ksenia asked, frowning at a gnarl in the threads.

Ulway cleared his throat. "Twenty," he managed.

"You don't seem that old."

Ulway rubbed his bulky shoulder. "So how old are you?"

"I just turned 18." Ksena pulled the rogue thread free and settled back into making her bracelet.

Ulway didn't know what else to say.

"Done," Ksenia announced after a while. She tied off the threads and trimmed the excess with a tiny set of cutters from her belt. She held up the finished product for Ulway to see.

When Ulway asked if he could hold it, she draped it across his thick palm.

"I can teach you how to make one," she said.

"It's okay. I can make one if I want to." He shuffled his chair closer to her. "Watch this." Ulway dropped his hands just below the surface of the table so only Ksenia could see.

One moment, there was only one bracelet, resting in his right hand. The next, an identical bracelet appeared in his left palm.

Ksenia's mouth dropped open. Ulway handed both bracelets to her, and she held them as if they were magic. "They're exactly the same," she said, not quite believing it. "How did you do that?"

Ulway blushed and squirmed in his seat. "I don't know, I just can."

"Wow," Ksenia said, "Like, wow! Ulway, that's so cool!"

"But you can't tell anyone," Ulway said, remembering the warning his aunt gave him every time he duplicated food or gas for the generator in the storage room. No one was supposed to know that he had this power. For his own safety, and the safety of the restaurant, too.

"Not even my mom?"

"No."

"Okay," Ksenia said. "I promise I won't." She took one of the bracelets and tied it around Ulway's wrist. "There. Now we both have one. To symbolise our promise. Secret." She tied off her own bracelet, then touched her wrist to his.

The bracelet was a thin band patterned in arrow-shaped lines of colour: blue followed by green, pink, purple, red. Ulway got caught up in its vibrance, running a finger over the tiny knots making up the bracelet. "Thank you," he remembered to say.

Ksenia's eyes crinkled happily. Then seeing someone past him, her face dropped into a frown.

Ulway turned in his chair. Ksenia's mom was standing halfway up the stairs, resting her bony hip against the rail. Her thin hands fluttered in front of her, gestures flowing too fast for Ulway to register.

When he turned back, Ksenia was signing in response. "I'll see you later, Ulway," she said. As she got up from the table, she touched her wrist to his: their secret.

A grin broke over his face.

Ksenia joined her mom and the two of them headed downstairs.

Ulway half-stood, then sat back in the chair. He shouldn't push his luck. Ksenia and her mom didn't invite him along, so he should stay here. He held up his hand, admiring the friendship bracelet. She let him keep it! Did that mean they were friends already?

Across the table, someone pulled a chair free and sat down. Ulway broke out of his daydream and said hi to Sophie.

"Hello Ulway," the elderly lady said. "That's a very nice bracelet you have."

"Yes," he replied, suddenly shy. "Ksenia made it."

"She made one of them, that's true." Sophie folded her hands on the table and stared at him.

Ulway shifted uncomfortably. "She made it."

Sophie nodded, a twinkle in her eye. "Ulway, my dear, I know that you have a secret. I saw you share that secret with Ksenia just now. I was wondering," she opened her hands, "how did you know it was okay to share it?"

Ulway blinked, taken aback. "I don't know, what you mean?" he said, his words jumbling.

Leaning forward, Sophie motioned him to do the same. "I have a secret too. I'm wondering if now is the time to share it. My secret could really help someone, but it could change how people see me. So that was why I asked." Sophie leaned back, and patted the table with her vein-backed hands.

"I told her because she was nice," Ulway admitted. "Maybe I shouldn't've."

"Don't worry. I won't tell anyone. You've done a wonderful job keeping the restaurant running. I'm sure your parents would be very proud of you."

Ulway ducked his head to hide the sudden rush of tears. His parents would be proud of him, he knew that. But hearing someone else say it was overwhelming.

He heard the chair push back, and when he looked up, Sophie was gone.

Log Entry 5:

He's mobilised the S.U.s—as if we're some army. I can't reach the others. We're still cut off. Communications blocked. I'm afraid to mess around too much in the system in case he finds out.

He's not the same. The years have made him cruel. We're locked inside our moving shells, carried along as he wrecks destruction up the coast.

The first time was a shock. He announced it, made sure all the S.U. cameras were fixed on the target—a lesson. The weapon incinerated a factory of some kind. An intense red ball on the heat monitor consumed the smaller orange readings—consumed them, the readings that were people.

Why is he doing this?

I can't get out.

I have to do something.

Chapter 8
Arissa in the Kitchen

"Well, it's awkward, if I'm being honest," Arissa told Victoria. "Isak's in the dorm, May and Lucas still in that single room. We're all trying not to ask, but of course we all want to know..."

"If it's permanent," Victoria finished the thought and sat back from the generator. "They probably don't even know right now."

"You're right," Arissa sighed. "I just wish there was more we could do. How's it looking?" she raised her eyebrows at the generator, which had filled the kitchen with grey smoke an hour earlier.

"It shouldn't short out now. If it does, we're in big trouble."

"No big troubles, please. Just small, manageable ones." Arissa leaned on the counter in the centre of the kitchen, massaging her temples. "Thanks for listening. I didn't mean to burden you with all of that."

"No, it's actually nice to be your confidante for once. We all know how close you and May are. But you can't really talk to her about this, can you?"

Arissa shook her head. "I have to be there for her, not probe the wound."

"Well I'm here anytime you need to rant," Victoria smiled, tightening the clamp over the reconstructed wires. "All done!"

"Thanks, Victoria."

Victoria hefted her toolbag. "Happy to help." She gave Arissa's shoulder a light tap and pushed through the swinging door into the dining area.

Arissa sighed again, allowing herself another minute to work the tension out of her forehead with her fingers. Victoria didn't know half of her worries. May and Isak's relationship troubles were casting a dull shadow over the summer. One of the trading caravans from the coast that usually came through around this time was nowhere to be seen. Even with the chickens and goat and garden, plus the hunting and gathering from the forest, the restaurant's food stores were lower than they'd ever been. Ulway duplicated as much as he could, but things sometimes got used up by accident, or started going bad. He couldn't duplicate a fresh apple from a rotten one.

And thinking of Ulway, her nephew was getting closer to the new girl. Too close. Arissa barely knew anything about Ksenia, or Catherine for that matter. And Ulway, usually so shy, was opening up to a stranger. If he told Ksenia about his duplicating powers, could it put him, and all of the residents, in danger? She would tell him to be careful. To run and hide at the cabin if something happened to the restaurant. She couldn't lose anyone else.

She never used to think this way. Before Pinot and Ed left, she would've welcomed new people into the restaurant community without suspicion. Her ability to see beneath people's intentions gave her confidence in who she could trust. But her ability was not as strong as it had once been, and the Grafter incident last fall had given her a harsher perspective of the world. It was not one she liked very much—but she had to live with it.

Before she could head downstairs to find Catherine, Sophie came into the kitchen.

"I thought you'd be in here," Sophie said.

Arissa pushed back her thoughts and focused on the older woman across the counter. "What do you need, Sophie?"

"Well, I have come to a decision. Your nephew helped me,

in fact. I wasn't sure if now was the right time."

"The right time for what?" Arissa asked.

Sophie winked one walnut-shell eyelid, and tapped her nose with her crooked index finger. "To tell you my secret."

Chapter 9
Pinot Gets a Lead

Sitting on top of a sleeping bag near her campfire, Pinot polished off a mix of rabbit meat and yarrow from the cooled cast iron pan she'd cooked them in. The sleeping bag, the pan, the flint she'd used to start the fire—she'd picked up all kinds of useful things over the summer, abandoned at Grafter camps or taken from the more dangerous ones once she'd dealt with them. She wore an oversized green jacket and two layers of pants. The nights were getting crisp around the edges, summer just about to tumble into fall.

Settled by the warm flames and pensively full, Pinot traced the infinity symbol tattooed on the inside of her wrist. She got it about a year before the Event, when she was 16. Shouldn't've been allowed. She'd just picked up her fake ID and wanted to do something really bad, so she swaggered into a tattoo parlour in the worst area of town, picked one of the cheapest designs in the flash book, and let a big woman with elaborate braids tattoo the simple black figure eight on the inside of her wrist.

She still lived with her parents at the time, so she kept the tattoo hidden. Even wearing a cheap digital watch over it, Pinot felt the thrill, knowing she had something secret, something dangerous underneath.

She left home and dropped out of school shortly after that. Hooked up with Miller and the gang, living as dangerously as she wished, without having to hide anything. Even though it was probably the worst time in her life, she'd spent years missing that sense of freedom.

Now, she had her own secret, dangerous life out in the woods. She sat by the fire, her fingerless glove lifting at the wrist just enough to clearly display the infinity symbol.

Life moves around a track, she thought as she traced it, circling back to themes and places. She'd learned a lot this time around, and the loop ahead didn't scare her. Still, she had some decisions to make about the upcoming winter: if she should go back to the cabin or if she should head to Summerland before the snow set in. Or, go back to *Ulway's*, take up the mantle of doctor once again, cut her losses.

What did she want, this next go around on the track of life?

Voices filtered through the trees, getting louder. Pinot scuttled away from her fire, staying low as she made her way up the small crag that provided shelter from the wind. She waited at the apex overlooking her transient camp. She breathed deeply to quiet her racing heart. The people nearby would see the campfire through the trees and be drawn in. She could sound them out from here, and if they were worthy, she would join them. If they were not...

"Over here!" one of the voices said, then was *shh*ed into silence.

A figure came through the trees and cautiously approached the fire. They were dressed in a three-quarter length coat with a shawl wrapped around their neck. The gold detailing glowed in the firelight. Their hair was up in a bun, burnished gold.

Pinot shifted, accidentally dislodging a branch underfoot. It rustled—too loud.

The figure at the edge of the campfire clapped their hands once and raised them, palms outward, towards where Pinot was hiding. Then, they brought their hands to a namaste at their chest. They approached the camp confidently, casting a cursory glance over the fire, the used cookware, the sleeping bag.

Pinot tried to back away but couldn't move. Whatever the

person had done had frozen her in place. She strained to turn towards the approaching figure but couldn't even shift her eyes.

The figure's footsteps drew closer and stopped. "Well, look who it is!"

Pinot heard another clap and felt her body relax. She took a deep breath, tipping forward as she refound her balance. The figure standing over her was familiar. "Lily?"

"Asin!" Lily called toward the trees. "It's alright, we know this one."

Another figure moved into the firelight. Shorter than Lily, Asin was broad-shouldered and wore a corduroy jacket with a fur-lined collar, his long black hair braided behind him. "Who's up there with you?" he asked, his voice a rich bass.

"An old friend." Lily gave Pinot a hand up. "I wasn't sure we'd cross paths with you again."

"Life's full of surprises," Pinot said seriously. She followed Lily down the crag, where the three of them settled by the fire.

"It's wonderful to see you again." Asin added a log to the dying flames. "When you left us, you were on your way west, I believe."

Pinot nodded, trying to keep her voice steady. "We didn't get far. Winter hit and we got stuck for a while. Ed...I think some people...I was out getting supplies and when I came back, our place was cleaned out, there were footprints leading away... Someone took him."

Asin and Lily matched eyes over the fire. "Took him? Why?"

Pinot shrugged, scraping her heel into the dirt.

"We've heard some rumours from Summerland, but nothing definite. Do you know where they went?"

Pinot shook her head. "What about you two, so far from camp—foraging?"

"We're on firewood duty." Lily gave a slight laugh. "No one else volunteered."

"We've got about a month to store up enough for the winter." Asin stretched his thick arms overhead.

"So no more foraging for now?" Pinot asked.

"For now," Lily said in their warm gravelly voice.

"I really can't judge." Pinot tucked her chilled hands into her coat pockets. "I've been living as a Grafter myself for a long time now. Scavenger without a home, isn't that what a Grafter is?"

"You could come back with us," Asin suggested. "Then you'd be a Forager instead. A scavenger with a home."

Pinot felt the pen lid in her pocket. "Julius already tried to convince me, last time. Showed me the underground shelters you built."

"Are you seriously going to winter in the woods just to prove a point?" Lily asked, quirking a thin eyebrow.

Pinot almost protested, then settled into a grim smile. "I guess."

The idea of joining the Forager camp was tempting. A safe, warm place to spend the winter. Pinot wondered if Julius's condition would still apply: winter shelter in exchange for her medical knowledge. Teaching people how to take care of each other. Framed that way, she could see how it surpassed her other options. And they'd feed her for her trouble.

"You can share the shelter with Julius and I," Lily offered. "I know you weren't very popular the last time you stayed with us, being an outsider. But give everyone a few weeks underground with only you to patch them up, and I think they'll come around."

"Do they know about my healing powers? I mean, my manifest," Pinot said, remembering Asin's preference for the term.

"No. Reah never told anyone else."

"I thought that would be best," Asin confirmed, "even though Phyllis was suspicious…"

As she listened to Lily and Asin talk, Pinot soaked in the familiar voices and names. She'd lived among the Foragers as a prisoner then as an equal. But Asin and Lily's presence around her fire also left a sour taste in her mouth. If she hadn't insisted on leaving the Forager camp last fall, would Ed still be sitting next to her, alive and well, passing notes?

The night-sounds of the forest and the fire crackling filled the silence. Asin passed around a bag of dried berries and nuts while Lily hand rolled a cigarette and lit it in the campfire.

Thinking over what Asin had said, Pinot cleared her throat. "You mentioned rumours from Summerland?"

Asin nodded. "You know Lorraine?"

Pinot thought back to a medical visit she'd made to the town a couple years before—so long ago, it didn't feel like her memory, more like a film she'd seen once. "Not sure."

"One of the early residents. She's next to the inn, running a new place called the Phone Book that keeps track of people's whereabouts. Travellers go to her if they need to find someone. And we've heard that some of the missing people may have been abducted." Asin let out a breath, gazed up at the stars. "Terrible things in the world."

Pinot gritted her teeth.

"She might have heard about Ed," Lily said, wreathed in herbal smoke. "Maybe he passed through Summerland at some point."

"Maybe." Pinot stared into the low fire. Orange flames danced over the glowing coals as they oscillated between black, bright red, and gold.

Asin took the bedroll from his pack and spread it out next to the fire. "You're welcome to stay with us for the winter, in any case. See you both in the morning." Settling into his sleeping bag with a yawn, Asin pulled the top of it over his face. He rolled over, his breathing almost immediately falling into the rhythm of sleep.

"I hope you don't mind," Lily said in a hushed voice.

The quiet words pulled Pinot's focus back to the present. "Nice to have company," she admitted.

Taking one last draw from the cigarette, Lily flicked it into the low flames. "Sorry about freezing you earlier."

"Bet it comes in handy on the wasteland."

Lily grimaced as they shook out their sleeping bag. "More

than I like to think about."

"Yeah."

"Why'd you settle here, anyway?"

Pinot picked out the faint glow from *Ulway's* over the silhouetted trees. "Better here than out there."

Stepping into their sleeping bag, Lily zipped it up, encasing themself in the warm waterproof material. "Reah would love to see you again."

"Stop twisting my arm," Pinot sighed as she threw some branches into the fire. "I might actually give in."

"Why not?" Lily sat down next to her. "Listen, I'm sorry about what happened to Ed. He was a good guy. But sulking around alone in the woods won't bring him back."

The dry branches crackled and kicked up sparks. Pinot clenched her hands.

"It's true," Lily continued. "Are you punishing yourself for what happened?" Their expression was steady, curious.

Disarmed, Pinot settled into the question and realised she was.

"You made choices that you thought were best at the time," Lily said softly. "You didn't know what was going to happen."

When Pinot didn't reply, Lily briefly gripped her shoulder. "You could make it to Summerland with time to spare, if you wanted." They didn't press the subject. They stretched back and rested their head on their backpack. After a while, they closed their eyes.

Pinot drew her knees into her chest and watched as the flames died down to coals.

Log Entry 9:

He knocked us out again, for a few days this time. I've been trying to find a way into the hibernation controls, but there's a high chance he's waiting for one of us to try, daring us to.

Maybe if I start with something simpler. Are any of the others making headway? I swing between frustration and hope, pacing this prison, getting nothing done. Every couple days, the siren goes off and I go under, then wake up bruised and fatigued and thirsty. But it can't be hopeless, there has to be a way…

I reviewed the data our S.U.s gathered when we were up north, before the Event. Even though I didn't find anything useful, it was comforting, going over lists of plant samples, polar bear sightings, daily temperatures, and efficiency readouts. Remembering when the worst thing we had to worry about was the monthly supply drop or mail getting delayed.

We don't seem to be moving. As long as we don't get put under, I'll have time to think of something. If only I wasn't so goddamn tired…

Chapter 10
May and the
Tiny Room

Lucas played at May's feet. The carpet in the dining hall was faded and worn, a perfect surface to run his bright plastic car over. Lucas pushed the car a little and giggled as it rolled to a stop. May stretched an arm over the empty chair back next to her. Someone had pulled three chairs into a line facing the fireplace. Ready for whatever Arissa had called her upstairs for. An intervention maybe? A brief surge of resentment washed over her. Her relationship with Isak wasn't anyone else's business.

Arissa, Sophie, and Isak came out of the kitchen, clustering in front of the row of chairs. "What's this all about?" May asked Arissa.

"Sophie has something she wants to tell you," Arissa said.

Taking her cue, Sophie moved to stand by the fireplace. Isak hesitated and then sat a couple seats over from May. As Arissa sat in the empty seat between May and Isak, her shoulders tensed.

At the same time, a hum of feelings swelled around May. She straightened up in her chair, her eyes widening as she looked from Arissa to Isak. "I can feel…"

Arissa nodded to Sophie. "Our powers are stronger."

"Yes," Sophie said. She was slight and frail, grey braids tucked up in a knitted toque. She wore a fuzzy white cardigan over another sweater and slacks, her small feet tucked into oversized slippers.

May was struck by the impression of strength emanating from Sophie. She had never noticed it before.

Recognizing May's astonishment, Sophie smiled. "As you can see, your powers, your ability to feel what those around you feel, to influence their emotions, they are at full strength now. This is unusual, yes?"

May nodded. She hadn't been able to sense people's feelings for a very long time: the hurricane under Arissa's calm exterior, Isak's pain spiking through her like needles, Lucas's quiet contentment radiating like a sun at her feet. It took her a moment to separate herself from the sea of feelings to focus on Sophie, strong and soft Sophie who could cover a fire with her body and not be consumed.

Sophie made a dramatic chopping gesture with one of her thin hands. In an instant, the sensations of the people around her fell away and May was left with only what her eyes saw, her hands touched, her heart felt. May gasped at the sudden emptiness. "You did that?"

"That's my secret," Sophie said. "My power allows me to dampen the abilities of others. Stop them from working, you see?"

"Have you always been able to? Since the Event?"

"Oh yes." Sophie folded her hands thoughtfully. "I didn't realise it at first, but living here with so many others, I came to understand it. It is a passive ability: even when I'm not thinking about it, the dampening effect emanates around me. Arissa and I have agreed that it might be a way to help with little Lucas here."

Sophie slowly lowered herself to the floor. Her knees cracked as she gently drove the toy car into Lucas's foot. Lucas loved the new game and laughed each time Sophie manoeuvred the car to "boop" against him.

"Wait a minute," Isak said. "You said the effect is constant. Is that why so many of us have been losing our abilities the past few years?"

"Not losing." Sophie looked up from the toy car. "But dampened, yes. There are some people I avoid on purpose and direct my power away from. Some I try to pass once a day to tone theirs down. Like yours, Isak."

Isak sat forward in his chair. "That's why I don't jump as much or as far as I used to?"

"That's exactly it." Sophie offered Lucas her crooked finger and smiled when he took it in his tiny hand. "Sometimes, it affects the wrong people. Pinot for instance. That was too bad. She slept in the same room as me, and I can't direct the dampening effect when I'm asleep. Plus, she made sure to check on me once a week after that nasty bout of bronchitis I had a couple winters ago."

"We needed her." May shook her head. "You should have told her!"

"Maybe." Raising herself to her knees, Sophie took Arissa's offered hand and returned to her feet. "Oh, thank you. Yes, maybe I should've told you all sooner. But it doesn't do harm. I try to maintain normalcy around here as much as possible. Soothe the more troublesome powers. Avoid the ones keeping us alive."

"Do you know everyone's abilities?" Arissa asked.

"I do." Sophie smoothed her cardigan before taking a seat next to the fireplace. "And I know how I can help." Sophie's blue eyes reflected the soft light coming in through the windows.

"With Lucas?" May bent down to bring him onto her knee.

"Lucas is the opposite of me. He can empathise with people's powers, make them stronger, use them himself. What would you call that, enhancing? Yes." Sophie nodded, pleased with the comparison. "So, he can travel through time with Isak or feel the emotions of others like May. As he grows older, he may learn to control his ability. Until then, there's the risk of him tagging along with dad."

"And you can stop that from happening?" Isak asked.

"I can. It's easy to arrange. I can visit Lucas throughout the week, manage his enhancing ability. We can discuss a schedule, places and times I can be around Isak as well. So, there it is!" Sophie released her folded hands and held them out to the group. "What do you think?"

May frowned. "Absolutely not."

"Oh for God's sake, May!" Isak exclaimed.

"Why not?" There was an edge in Arissa's voice. "It's a reasonable solution."

May winced as Isak and Arissa's disappointment washed over her. She'd forgotten how poignant other people's emotions were. Sophie was directing the dampening effect away from her, to let their emotions impact her decision. But it wouldn't change her mind.

"Your power dampens, you said," May addressed Sophie. "Lucas is so young. Your dampening might harm his development. You don't know. Your power could slowly be poisoning us all. If that were the case, would you tell us?"

"May—" Isak interjected.

"You didn't tell us about controlling our powers before, so why would you tell us anything else? How dare you decide what's best for us!" May gripped Lucas to her chest.

Lucas whined and arced in her arms, reaching back for the car on the floor.

"I've heard enough." May didn't wait for their responses. She carried her wailing son down the stairs, his cries echoing down the dim hallway as she brought him into their room. She closed the door and leaned her back against it, steadying herself against the cool painted wood.

Lucas's cries softened to a whimper.

"I'm sorry," she said and gave him a quick kiss on the forehead. Placing him into the crib, she distracted him with one of the handmade stuffed animals. She changed his cloth diaper, dropping the sullied one into a lidded bin. After washing her hands in the basin by the door, she sat on the edge of the old mattress and waited until Lucas laid down, babbling sleepily at the stuffed animal under his arm.

May lay out on the bed. Her thoughts whirled. The dose of her old power had thrilled her more than she liked to admit. She hadn't realised before how much she missed it. How dare Sophie take it away from her! Sophie didn't have the right.

May felt herself veering into the old emotional rut, the one that had ruined her friendship with Pinot—the way of suspicion, and hatred, and self-righteousness. She'd thrived off that intoxicating poison, not realising that it was destroying something precious. She didn't want that feeling to take over her life again. But when she raised her hands above her, they shook with anger. This place was all wrong and she wanted to leave it behind. But there was nowhere to go. Not alone with a baby. She would have to stay.

An echo of Isak's pain pinged through her. It wasn't his fault, skipping through time. And what little control he had was because of Sophie's power. May hated that she kept losing him during these little marital skirmishes. She couldn't seem to stop losing him, couldn't stop driving him away. But what else could she do for him? What other way could she keep Lucas safe?

A no-win situation. It wasn't fair. In the tiny room, she was cut off from the emotional hum of humanity around her. Completely alone.

Chapter 11
Ulway and Ksenia
Make a Plan

Ulway met Ksenia in the downstairs gaming room. The open area was comfortably crowded with small tables, worn armchairs, and plenty of natural light coming in through the generous windows framing the forest beyond. It was a quiet space for the most part, a little-used foosball table crammed next to the out-of-tune piano. Encyclopaedias filled a low shelf by the defunct pop machine. It was a place people came to read or think or nap when the rest of the restaurant was too loud.

Ulway wiped his palms on his sweater. Ksenia was waiting for him on the long bench-like couch with a throw pillow held over her stomach.

"Here's your spot," she said, hitting the section of cushion next to her.

Ulway sat on the edge of the couch, then shuffled back. His knee accidentally knocked against hers.

Ksenia touched their bracelets together, their usual greeting. "I used to live far away," she said.

"How far?" Ulway asked.

"Days and days. But I know the way. I made notes in my head and turned them into a song. I remember exactly how to get back."

"Oh." Ulway's stomach dropped.

Ksenia shook her head. "I'm saying I could go back. If I

wanted."

"Do you?"

After a moment, she nodded. "It's way more fun than here. There are lots of people our age, and younger. And always babies. There's a party whenever there's a baby. And we have some cows and fields. It's really fun."

"So why'd you leave?"

"Dunno," Ksenia puffed up her hair. "Mom said we had to."

"Oh." Ulway didn't know what else to say.

"Would you come with me? If I went back?"

Ulway's palms got really sweaty. "Uhhh…."

"You don't have to answer. I just thought you might like it there. You could pet the cows, they're nice."

"Oh," Ulway said, uncertain. "I would like that."

"You would?" Ksenia's face lit up. "I hoped you would! We could go and then come back. We wouldn't have to stay. You could meet all my friends."

"Yeah," Ulway smiled. "Okay."

"And they'd really think your powers are cool. They might even throw you a party!"

The idea of having a party thrilled Ulway. The restaurant held a big feast around the New Year and made little cakes on someone's birthday, but those weren't parties. He remembered the extravagant birthday parties and weddings his parents used to host at the restaurant.

"When do you want to go?"

Ksenia shuffled closer to him. "We should leave soon. Before it gets cold. We'll have to put away some extra food for the trip and bring blankets and stuff."

"Okay," Ulway said, excited and scared and happy all at once.

"Don't tell anyone," she said, holding out her bracelet.

"I promise." Ulway touched his wrist to hers.

Chapter 12
Rhonda and the Archive

Arissa led Rhonda down the stairs and past the two chairs making a little sitting area at the bottom. She unlocked a door on the left, one that hadn't been opened in some time. Rhonda went in after her. The air inside was stuffy, heavy with dust and nostalgia. Three server towers stood on the bottom of a messy shelving unit covered in cords, disks, and computer parts. Ed's old office.

Arissa reached up to the top shelf and took down a file box. She set it gingerly on the corner of the desk and brushed the dust from her hands. "This is what I wanted your help with," Arissa said, leaning a hip against the desk. "A few years ago, I thought that starting an archive of people's experiences on the wasteland and their memories of life before the Event would be something worth doing. Ed provided a lot of journal material, I got some notes and files from the others. But things around here," she shook her head with a smile. "They are never easy. I didn't have the time to go through them. So here they are, all these bits of life with nowhere else to go. I thought you would be the person to ask about continuing this project, if you're interested? I've seen you with your camera, I know how much you value stories and people's lives. Do you think you'd be up for it?"

Joy flooded over Rhonda. "Really? Me, catalogue all this, add to it, make it something to stand the test of time?"

"You sound excited about the idea."

"Oh, I really am!" Rhonda reached for the box. Then, she remembered the dust. "Are any of the materials on the server?" she asked instead, waiting to open the box until she could sweep it off outside.

"You'll have to look into it. I can give you use of the generator between three and four every afternoon except Sundays," Arissa said. "We can run an extension cord down for you."

Rhonda could barely contain her excitement at the thought of extra computer time.

"I can work with that."

"Fantastic," Arissa said and passed her the office key. "It's all yours."

A Note on Summerland

In Year 6, Summerland was the largest settlement in the area we now call the Western Wastes. The population averaged about 50 people. In the summer, workers and travellers called "transients" kicked the population up to 80 or even 100. In the fall, the numbers went back down since there wasn't a lot of work or extra food in the winter.

The settlement's permanent residents had stable homes with thick walls and watertight roofs. The half a dozen workshops and cottages, along with the vineyard, comprised the original patch that had survived the Event. The residents took care of the vineyard, cultivated it, and lived off of the grapes and hardier plants, eventually establishing trade routes to surrounding communities.

By Year 6, the old-world buildings were only a small part of the settlement. They lined the southeast side of Main Street which led up to the town courtyard. The work office was the cornerstone of the courtyard, sandwiched between a storagehouse and the school. There were around six kids attending the school at this time. After class, they would stop at the Juice Bar on the other side of Main Street where they would trade an hour of work for a cup of grape juice. Work and food were Summerland's currency.

Every morning, the office assigned community projects— patching the school roof, cleaning debris off the road, carting human waste to the dump site outside of town, or working a shift in the community garden. Most of the permanent residents spent all day tending to the vineyard, so these odd jobs fell to transients. Competition for work, which paid in room and board in the tenement housing on the southwest corner of town, was intense. If you didn't work, you didn't eat.

There were some exceptions to the hard split of resident/transient. Someone had to manage the inn for the trade caravans. There was also the Phone Book, which Lorraine ran next door. For a fee, anyone could inquire about a missing relative or friend. Lorraine would consult her records and provide their last known location. Travellers could trade information to reduce the cost of using her records, but they always had to come willing to pay something...

Chapter 13
Lorraine and the Visitor

Lorraine was deep in her index card system when a stranger pushed past the tarp hanging over the doorway. *Kind of familiar*, Lorraine thought, setting aside her metal card box to study them. The stranger had short dark hair with a patch of white, scarring around the left eye, light brown skin, dark brown eyes. Shorter than average, not muscular, but unusually healthy-looking for a transient. Lorraine wondered if they would tell her their name.

"Welcome," she smiled up at them, "who can I help you find today?"

The visitor ran a weary hand over their closely-cropped hair. They formed a word, then they shook their head.

"It's okay." Lorraine was used to that kind of reaction. She offered people hope, and hope was a devastating thing. "Come around the desk, there's a seat back here for you. We can take this slow."

The visitor didn't make eye contact but moved to take the padded stool next to a low wooden table. Lorraine backed her chair out from the desk, manoeuvring the thin silver wheels until she was facing the visitor at a comfortable distance. The table between them was already set with a couple of blank index cards and a scattering of pencil stubs.

"If you want to write it out, if it's easier?" Lorraine said after a bit of silence had passed. "I can read English, French, or

Spanish."

The visitor nodded.

"I need to know their name, a basic description. We can go from there."

"Okay," the visitor managed, and picked up a pencil.

As they wrote, Lorraine took in more of their appearance, intending to add it to her records. They seemed to be in their early to mid-20s. Clothing was a green jacket over a well-worn hoodie, long pants, hiking boots. A grey backpack that used to be black, bleached from outdoor living.

The visitor finished writing and slid the index card towards her.

Lorraine rolled forward so that her shins rested against the edge of the low table. "Now," she said with a weight in her voice, "This is your first time in here, I think, so it's important that I show you how this works." She pulled a filled-out index card from the armrest pocket of her chair and placed it on the table in front of the visitor.

The visitor leaned forward to squint at it, then frowned.

"It's a shorthand form that only I know how to read," Lorraine explained. "My records cannot be stolen or copied. In case you came in here with any ideas."

"If I did," the visitor flashed a sharp grin, "you've banished them from my mind."

"Perfect. As for payment—"

The visitor fished in their hoodie pocket and tossed a single handmade cigarette onto the table.

Lorraine recognized it—yellowed paper, mild herbal scent, a double fold to secure the seam. Lily's work. The visitor knew the Foragers, then. Interesting.

Keeping her face neutral, Lorraine accepted the visitor's payment with a nod, sweeping the cigarette and the index card up together. "I'll see what I have." Returning to the desk, Lorraine compared the visitor's query to her 'phone book' system.

The visitor's knee shook as Lorraine flipped through the

metal index card box.

Lorraine cross-checked the description against every viable match, but came up empty. "I'm sorry," she said to the visitor. "I'm afraid there's nothing on file."

Gripping their knees, the visitor let out a shuddering sigh.

Lorraine hesitated, then continued. "I'll tell you what. Are you staying in town? You paid me already, so I can flag your query—if anyone reports someone matching your description, I'll let you know."

The visitor's expression cleared. "I'll be around."

Lorraine felt another glimmer of recognition, the sense she'd seen this visitor before. "Do you come to Summerland often?" she asked, trying to connect the face with a name. From a couple of years ago, maybe? She sifted through her memory, but she didn't have a particular talent for remembering faces. That's what the index cards were for. And she saw so many people—

"Can I make another inquiry?" the visitor asked, dodging her question. They scratched some words on another blank card and offered it along with a handful of dried fruit. "Her name's Irene."

Lorraine checked her records. She waved the offering away. "Today's not your day, I'm afraid. Doesn't seem like anyone's seen her."

"Makes sense," the visitor smiled to themself. They pocketed the fruit and went out into the street.

Pestered by the elusive sense of familiarity, Lorraine busied herself with erasing the visitor's scratchy handwriting and updating her own records. To the first card, "Ed", she added the date and nature of inquiry, slotting it in the "Ongoing" section of her filing box. She wrote up a new card for "Irene." And when she finally gave up and checked the visitor's appearance against her 'phone book,' everything fell into place. Scarring around the left eye, white patch in dark hair, physical impression of health and stamina—the visitor had been to Summerland two years before, a doctor doing her rounds. Name: "Pinot."

Lorraine tucked the card away and considered crossing the courtyard to let Louis know. He liked to keep tabs on people of interest staying in Summerland. But the office didn't have a ramp and she didn't feel like sitting out in the early fall chill waiting for Louis to make time for her. Besides, she'd logged Pinot's visit in her records, which she would tell him, if he ever bothered to check in with her. What kind of brother was he, anyway?

She indulged in feeling unappreciated for a moment, then snapped her index card box shut. "Doesn't matter to me what a doctor's doing in town," she announced. Her mind finally at ease, Lorraine turned her attention to picking apart the newest poem by ECB.

A Note on ECB,
Summerland's First Poet

Summerland's first and greatest poet was only known by their initials: ECB.

Their poems appeared on scraps of fabric, on sheets of plywood, scratched into metal cups or on the backs of defunct tablets. Haikus, sonnets, lyrics—any form, any medium. All were in touch with Summerland's daily life, from vineyard scenes to transients-for-hire crowding the work office doorway.

These poems were read and passed through town. It became a nightly pastime at the Juice Bar to read the poems aloud or have contests to see who could recite them from memory. Summerland welcomed these nearly-anonymous works with enthusiasm: they gave people something to talk about.

When they first started to appear, the poems would circulate into obscurity. They'd get discarded, or taken away by a traveller who wanted a familiar voice to carry with them into the wasteland. After a while, a resident named Samir started to collect them. When a poem got tired, or was replaced by something new, Samir took it to his cabinet. Residents could visit the cabinet freely at any time. A couple of rival collectors rose up in town throughout the years, but Samir had community recognition.

The source of the poems was a subject of town interest as well. As the years went on, candidates for the mysterious poet dwindled to a list of around three. Community gossip had long favoured Jesse Sr., but after he passed away and the poems continued uninterrupted, Elanora became the new number one contender. Some were in the Manu camp; some were convinced they had spotted Al scratching something into the side of a dented garbage bin, but no one could be sure.

In any case, the poems gave Summerland, the only town of note in the Western Wastes at that time, its sense of continuing identity. Of course, there were other poets, but none so well-known and loved as the rogue ECB. To this day, no one knows who they really were.

Chapter 14
Isak After the Rain

Isak fidgeted with his medic-alert bracelet as he waited for May.
Puddles surrounded the log bench in the woods; rain dripped
from the trees. A spider web on the raspberry bush across from
him was speckled with water droplets that caught sunlight as the
rain clouds blew west. Stationary on the bench, Isak reeled from
the speed of the clouds, rushing overhead like giant ships, an
armada of black and grey and gold sails. Lost in the movement,
he started when May sat down on the other end of the bench.

"Hey," he said and cast a quick glance over. May was
immobile, her red-rimmed eyes fixed on the spider web. His
throat closed, he could barely get the next words out. "How are
you doing?"

"Fine." The bitterness in her voice ripped through his chest.

"I, uh…" Isak pressed his hand against the log under him,
the bark imprinting into his fingers. "I wanted to talk to you
about something."

"Go ahead."

"I'm going to ask Sophie to dampen my powers," Isak
managed. "I already sleep in the same room as her, so it
shouldn't make much of a difference."

"It's your body."

"Can I say something?"

May let out an impatient breath. "Yes."

Isak sat up a little straighter, gripping his hands in his lap. He'd rehearsed this part, but suddenly his mouth was dry. "I've been thinking about what's happening between us, and…how it might be part of a pattern? Uh…" Isak swallowed. "We've been together for a long time, and I think I know you pretty well." Isak turned to face her, keeping his voice gentle. "You tend to set up opponents. Something to strive against. After the Event, you fought the isolation and the loneliness tooth and nail, for both our sakes. You kept us alive. When Jax showed up, took us captive, you wanted to protect Pinot. But when Jax was gone, you needed someone to fill that spot. Pinot, who you felt guilty about, was a perfect target. And the past while…it's been me. I never noticed the pattern, until recently. I've always known you were strong and principled. I admire those things about you. I just…never thought you'd choose me to strive against."

May glared at him. "I didn't choose you!"

"Not consciously. That's not what I mean…"

"What do you mean then?"

Isak sighed. "I shouldn't've brought it up."

"No, I want to know what you think. You're the academic one, right?"

"May…Every conversation doesn't have to be a fight. We can figure this out. Everyone believes we can."

"That doesn't matter," May said. "Do *we* believe we can? I don't think I do."

Isak grasped at her words, trying to understand. "What…"

"I think you know as well as I do that this isn't working."

"But Lucas…"

"If you're spending time with Sophie, you won't be able to jump. Just promise me you won't take Lucas near her."

"Now you're making Sophie the enemy."

May gestured tiredly. "Enemies, friends, lovers. I've finally realised that it doesn't matter. I'm alone, and Lucas is all I have." She got up from the bench. "I'm sorry, Isak," she said before walking back up to the restaurant.

Chapter 15
Pinot in Summerland

Pinot left the Phone Book. She ran a hand along her head, the short hair bristling against her palm. She'd thought cutting her hair would be enough to keep her presence in Summerland a secret: the last thing she needed was to be swarmed by residents who recognized her as the "doctor" who used to heal pneumonia and stave off infection. It had been a couple of unkind years since she'd been through Summerland. Hopefully, the changes in her appearance would be enough to keep her presence in town unnoticed.

Main Street led her down to the southwest sector, the neighbourhood of transients. She leaned against the side of a shack, lighting one of the cigarettes Lily had given to her as a good luck gift. It was all shambles and ramshackle in the tenements: most of the shacks were made of wood pallets covered over with tarps and old blankets with sheet metal tacked around doorways or used to mark out little yards of dirt. Most of the places were split into four on the inside, just enough room in each for someone to lie down. That's what you got for working in the community, fixing the roofs of the permanent houses across the street or whatever odd jobs they had available at the work office. Most of the shacks would be empty, but in the height of summer, they'd be packed full of Grafters and travellers trying to eke out a living.

Pinot took a draw and felt the knot in her chest relax. The cigarette was minty, pleasant. It was nothing like pre-Event smoking, but she couldn't quite remember what tobacco had tasted like—her brain interchanged the recalled aftertaste with the acrid grittiness of old coffee. The pounding of her pulse in her ears slowed and slipped under the sounds around her: a loose flap of metal rattled slightly in the wind. Distant voices echoed down Main Street. Shuffling from a cluster of shacks further in, low voices, the bright arc of water being poured.

She'd have to stay, she decided. Lorraine would tell her if there was any news of Ed—Summerland was the only major hub left, surely someone would come through with tales of a red-haired man who could control electricity. Yes, here in the heart of the wastes, that's where she should be. Biding her time. Ready to jump on a lead when it appeared. Lily was right. Hiding out in the woods wouldn't help her find Ed.

A couple walked between the shacks. They leaned against a tacked together fence separating the worn dirt path and what looked like a makeshift shower stall, their shoulders touching.

Pinot finished the cigarette and let the end crumble out of her fingers. She took a deep breath of fresh, cool air. Then, she went over to the couple.

One was dressed in a brown coat fitted to their slim build, their honey-brown hair shaved along one side, their cheeks bright red from the fall chill. The other one was taller, with brown skin, a thick beard, and short black hair. They were dressed in a battered duster jacket and had a tension to their broad shoulders that put Pinot on her guard.

"What's Summerland like these days?" Pinot asked when they both shifted to allow her a leaning place on the fence.

"To be honest, we haven't been here that long ourselves," the one in the fitted brown coat said. "But pleasant enough."

"Caden," the other growled.

"Oh relax, Jeff." Caden said, putting an arm around Jeff's waist. "He's still distrustful of strangers."

Jeff studied Pinot, then grunted. "Haven't seen you around

before. Grafter?"

Pinot shrugged. "So what if I am? You look like you've seen your share of wasteland living."

Jeff shared an amused look with Caden. "Sure."

Keeping a casual tone, Pinot kicked her heel against the fence. "If you haven't been in Summerland long, where'd you come from? You were both Grafters before?"

"I was," Jeff said after a tense moment. "Caden...he was settled somewhere, temporarily."

"Oh yes, I lived in a *mobile home*," Caden smiled, showing his even, white teeth.

"That's really good," Jeff chuckled. "Mobile home."

Pinot stiffened, gripping the rough fence with her bare fingers. "What did you say your names were?"

Picking up on her body language, Jeff broadened his shoulders. "Do we know you?"

"Mobile home," Pinot said in a low voice. "As in, *Survival Unit.*"

"Holy shit!" Caden gasped. "You. At that camp in the wasteland. You're the one who knew Jax."

Pinot pushed off from the fence then turned to face them. The last time they'd crossed paths, Jeff and Caden were encased in Survival Units they'd been taking west. "Did you find him?"

"Fucker double-crossed us," Jeff growled.

"He took everything we had and made off with the SUs," Caden continued. "It took us a week to find food after that. Eventually, we made it here."

Pinot's shoulders slumped. "I should've warned you."

"Why would you?" Jeff relaxed. "We didn't really give you a chance. Maybe," he slid his free hand around Caden's waist, "if I'd listened to a stranger, we could've stayed out of that mess."

"Wow, look at us, learning to trust again!" Caden teased.

Pinot settled back against the fence.

"Are you looking for a place to stay?" Jeff asked.

"Yeah," Pinot said. "Work-to-live, right? Who do I talk to?"

"Don't worry about tonight," Caden said, "there's space in

ours, you can sign up at the work office in the morning."

"Alright," she said, crossing her arms. "Thanks."

"What was your name, again?" Jeff scratched at his beard. "Something like, I dunno. What was it, Caden?"

Caden stared into the grey sky. "Pinot. Is that right?"

Pinot hesitated. "Can you call me something else? I don't want people to know I'm around."

"Sketchy, but okay," Caden smiled. "Whatever you want."

The name came to her, a leaf caught in the flow of the forest stream, reaching her just as she said it: "Yarrow."

"For what it's worth," Jeff said as he and Caden led the way to their tenement shack, "Welcome to Summerland."

Chapter 16
Ulway's Plan is Discovered

Ulway knew that something was wrong when his aunt pulled him away from washing dishes. "I need to talk with you," was all she said as she led the way out of the kitchen. She pushed open the door to their room and gestured for him to go in. The hard glare in her eyes, the way her mouth pressed into a frown. Something was definitely wrong.

He sat on his cot. Arissa motioned to someone down the hall and after a moment, Catherine and Ksenia entered. They sat on Arissa's bed across from him.

Arissa lowered herself next to Ulway, the cot springs screeching in the heavy silence of the room.

"Ulway," Arissa said, keeping her face turned to Catherine. "I found a stash of food under your bed."

Ulway grimaced.

"Catherine also found a cache of supplies in Ksenia's backpack. Can you tell me what's going on here?"

Ksenia caught Ulway's eyes and shook her head. Noticing this, Catherine signed something to her. Ksenia hung her head, her hands upturned in her lap.

"Ulway," Arissa said. "Were you planning on leaving?"

"No!" Ulway said, horrified. "I would never leave you! Why would you ask me that?"

"But you wanted to go on a trip?"

Ulway deflated. "Yes."

"Were you going to tell me?"

Twisting the bracelet around his wrist, Ulway didn't respond.

"This is very serious." His aunt put a hand on his bulky shoulder. "You know that you're needed here."

"I never get to do anything!" he cried, pulling away. "People don't even know what I can do! If I went to the colony, they would throw me a party!"

"A party?" Arissa looked over to Catherine, who shook her head. "Ulway, the people where Ksenia used to live would not throw you a party. They would most likely hurt you and force you to do things for them."

"No!"

Catherine stood up. Ksenia signed something, but her mother ignored her. Instead, Catherine untucked her shirt and lifted it to reveal that her stomach was covered in old cuts and circular burn marks.

Ulway and Ksenia both gasped.

"Catherine explained it all to me," Arissa said. "She gave me permission to tell you so that you won't go to that place."

Ksenia stared at her mother, shocked.

"The colony is very rigidly structured. People over 18 are forced to get married and have babies as soon as possible. Catherine wanted to protect Ksenia from the cruel man who wanted to marry her. That's why Catherine made them run away."

"It's not true!" Ksenia said, signing aggressively as Catherine steadily tried to interrupt with gentle signs of her own. "It can't be!"

"Ulway," Arissa drew his attention. "Promise me you will never go there."

Shaken by the story and trying not to watch Ksenia and Catherine's confusing exchange, Ulway nodded.

"Good." Arissa hugged him to her side in a fierce and quick embrace.

Chapter 17
Rhonda Reads

Rhonda laid out the scraps of paper on the wood-grained dining hall table. Hundreds of them, scrawled on receipt paper, notebook slips, edges of phone book pages, the backs of soup labels. All bundled together with crumbly elastics or in yellowing sandwich bags. Out of order, scattered through years and most of them undated. Rhonda considered them in the order she took them out, figuring that would be the best way to start. The closest thing she had to authorial intent.

Reading someone else's private thoughts was strange. She treated Ed's notes and history as some kind of coherent text. Maybe that was the wrong way to go about it. Whatever Ed had intended by writing them, he didn't know he was writing for an audience. There were musings, stories, plenty of things Rhonda had no context for—his life before the Event, the convenience store, the Survival Units.

Once Ed arrived at the restaurant, though, his writing changed. He was more sure of himself, more aware of his own shortcomings and flaws, and there was a real narrative movement to what before had been stream-of-consciousness, disjointed, opaque. His descriptions of daily life at the restaurant were in line with what Rhonda saw around her, yet evoked a feeling of awe that she hadn't considered before. She loved filming the mundane for what it was, capturing little moments that often went unseen. Ed infused these moments with a kind of wonder, acknowledging the miracle that all these things still existed. Even something as simple as a teaspoon was not outside his realm of description.

There were also dozens more ideas for his Interactive Fiction game. Rhonda had played through all the levels of *Trace of Shadows* that Ed had made before he left. The first time she sat down to play it was also the first time she and Nick hung out together. She was nostalgic about the game; it made her sad, knowing that so much of it was left unmade. That was one reason, at least, to make the archive more accessible: maybe someday, someone would come along who would know how to finish the game. Even for that small reason, it was worth doing.

She focused on the slips of paper, shifted some around as she read the cramped handwriting. The way Ed wrote about people was interesting, too. He'd known Arissa for years, had more insight into May and Isak's relationship than they maybe would've liked to know. And his love for Pinot was clear in every word he wrote about her. Recording something she said, describing her brooding over a cup of coffee in the clinic. Had he ever told Pinot how he felt? Did he even know?

"Those are Ed's notes," May said.

"Yeah." Rhonda looked up as May reached her. "Arissa said I could run the archive, since…well, I hope it's okay with you. I know you were friends."

May nodded, her mouth pressed in on itself. Her hand reached across the spread out pages and picked up a piece of receipt paper. "He was our only friend for a while. Before we knew that more people had survived. I…" May carefully replaced the paper, squaring the edges to the notes around it. "I'm glad you're reading them." She left Rhonda alone, her footsteps fading down the stairs.

Rhonda read until the light from the dining room windows turned grey. She decided to spend her hour on the computer each day typing up the notes. She could save them on the spare USB she'd found in the office's jumble of cords and computer parts as a backup in case something happened to the originals.

Rhonda layered the scraps of paper in the sandwich bags (without the old elastics), and doubly-sealed them inside a tupperware bin she'd salvaged from the shed. The bin used to hold trowels and gloves, some other odds and ends for gardening. She'd swapped it with a crate from the kitchen, and so far no one had been the wiser. She found a piece of painter's tape and labelled the bin with a dying sharpie: *Archive 1 - Ed's Notes*. She'd have to find another container for *Archive 2 - Misc* when she got to it, but transcribing Ed's messy handwriting would be time-consuming enough.

The idea that had been germinating since Arissa gave her access to Ed's office pushed up into her thoughts. After she typed up a copy of what she already had, she should expand the archive: add stories from the people at the restaurant, records of their journeys, how they got where they were now. She could make the archive something everyone was a part of. Scenes and images cut together into one overarching narrative.

Rhonda knew that even if no one read the archive, if it all stayed neatly organised in a plastic bin, it was worth doing for herself. A creative project to keep her focus clear and her energies engaged. Something fulfilling to take the edge off of the hard reality they were living in.

"Good," she confirmed. She picked up the bin and headed downstairs.

Log Entry 13:

We've started moving east. I'm working on a way to override the hatches. Once we reach Summerland, I'll open them. He won't destroy the one settlement that offered him help when no one else would. Summerland should be safe.

But if we all leave, who will look after the data? The S.U.s might hold the only viable readings about the Event and how it changed the world—literally changed the make-up, the atmosphere, the soil composition. It might be the key to understanding what happened to us. And he doesn't care—not anymore.

I can't let anything happen to it.

Chapter 18
Yarrow

"I'm back," Pinot announced. She pushed aside the sheet of corrugated aluminium serving as a door, her bare fingertips sticking slightly to the cold metal. The tiny entry area was empty. Pinot stripped off her toque, green jacket, and topmost pair of pants, dropping them in the laundry bin.

Jeff lifted the corner of the tarp blocking off his and Caden's side of the shack. "So?"

"Exactly what it sounds like," Pinot replied, putting on her clean fingerless gloves. "Carting shit is shit."

"But…?" Jeff prompted.

"I got double rations."

"Right."

Pinot sighed and ducked under the low doorway to her room, a six by four foot closet half the size of the room Caden and Jeff shared. Just enough space to roll out her sleeping bag and sit her backpack in the corner. She'd tacked one of her tarps from her summer in the woods along the walls to improve insulation, but it was still too cold. It was only November—she hated to think what full winter would be like. But at least she wasn't in a place on her own. Jeff and Caden had insisted she stay, all of them knowing that more bodies in the shack would lead to more collective heat.

She was glad for another reason: if she hadn't been around

to spike Caden's drinks with her healing spit, his light cough would've deepened into bronchitis by now. She found herself healing on the sly, bringing food to tenement dwellers with head colds, spitting in the communal teapot when no one was looking. No one knew about her powers in the tenements—but here she was, using them anyway.

She sat cross-legged on her sleeping bag, taking sips from her canteen to wash out the memory of chamber pots and piss bottles and buckets. "Carting shit" was the one job at the work office that was available every single day—and the only one that offered double rations.

She was partnered with a tall woman named Lauren. Pinot didn't start a conversation and Lauren didn't care. They pulled the fat plastic barrel around Summerland on a flat cart, stopping at the work office, the school, the Juice Bar, and the inn. Pinot kept her head down, the toque pulled low over her forehead, but no one looked too closely at the transients taking their shit away, and no one recognized her.

When they reached the clinic, Pinot pretended that she'd forgotten her gloves at the inn and rejoined Lauren after the clinic was taken care of. At noon, all of the tenement residents came to the courtyard to empty their piss buckets. On the way down Main Street, they stopped at each of the half-dozen old world buildings for the permanent residents to add their shit to the collective haul. Then, Pinot and Lauren took the cart into the wind-swept ice-encrusted wasteland just south of the tenement neighbourhood, found the bright red post, and dumped the barrel's contents.

"That's it," Lauren said as they watched the town's refuse spread and sink into the thin sheet of snow.

Pinot laughed, and Lauren joined in until tears ran down both of their faces.

They'd returned to the work office and parted in silence.

A slight cough came from outside the shack. The sheet metal whined as someone opened the door. "Hey Yarrow, are you here?"

Pinot crawled over to the entry to her room and pulled the tarp aside.

"You survived!" Caden cheered, half in and half out of the shack.

Jeff stuck his feet into the entryway as he tied on his hiking boots.

"Come on, we're going out!"

"Out?" Pinot said, not understanding. Outside was cold and it was starting to get dark. Still, she pulled an extra sweater from her bag, expecting a quick hike to the tea hut a few shacks down.

Jeff had already joined Caden on the path outside. "All here," Jeff announced as Pinot reached them. Caden and Jeff turned up Main Street, playfully kicking bits of snow at each other until Caden jumped on Jeff's back and they went, laughing, up to the courtyard.

Pinot followed at a distance. Usually when she went up to the work office she wore a slouchy toque to hide the white patch in her hair. The sweater she had on didn't even have a hood. She could go back for her hat—

Caden and Jeff called for her from up the street. Whatever they had planned, she hoped it wouldn't involve the clinic.

"After you!" Caden gestured to the Juice Bar with an overly-dramatic bow.

"We spent all morning bottling the stuff," Jeff grinned through his beard. "And that comes with some added perks. Plus, you have double rations, right?"

"You planned this?" Pinot crossed her arms.

"Sure did!" Caden pulled her inside. "You're going to love it."

The Juice Bar was the most solid building Pinot had been in since leaving *Ulway's*. The floor was made of jigsawed wooden slats, the walls a mix of wood panelling and stone and mortar work—a little eclectic at best, but cosy. The seating, though, was the most stunning part of all. Smooth faux leather bar stools and iron work chairs spotted the room around actual tables, half of them surrounded by groups of residents and transients. A rounded bar took up an entire side of the room, with a person the size and shape of a wine cask positively glowing behind it.

"There they are!" the bartender bellowed as he waved Caden and Jeff to the bar. "Come on lads, have a glass on me! And your friend there, come on up. What'll ya have?"

Pinot sat on the high bar stool next to Jeff. "What are my choices?"

The bartender laughed. "Only two choices here, and both of them grape."

"We'll have the good stuff," Caden winked.

"Of course you will!" The bartender laughed again and spread three glasses across the bar, pouring thick burgundy wine into each from a clay decanter.

"Is this one of the original buildings?" Pinot took one of the glasses.

"Not quite!" the bartender said, secreting the decanter under the counter. "Made of bits and pieces, some found materials, some donations from the residents. Does the trick though, doesn't it?"

"Cheers!" Caden said, clinking his glass against Pinot's and then Jeff's.

"Enjoy!" The bartender moved to help another patron down the curve of the bar.

Pinot savoured the rich wine, thinking of the grapes that had been grown, picked, and crushed to make the small portion in her glass.

Caden and Jeff moved off to join the poetry reciting contest, while Pinot used one of her rations to get another glass of the good stuff. She felt warm and comfortable in the hum of conversations in the low-lit room.

She was ready to finish her drink and go home to let herself be drawn down into the heavy warmth of her body when someone got up on the stool next to her. Their brown and grey hair stuck straight up from their rumpled forehead as if they had just been electrocuted. "As I live and possibly exist!" they exclaimed. "Pinot! How are ya?"

Pinot ground her teeth.

"Maybe you don't remember me? Clem? Last time you were here, I was working on that tetanus booster pill!" Clem threw their thick arm around Pinot's neck as if they were best friends. "I'm pleased to report that we're tetanus-free here in Summerland, yes indeed! A real breakthrough for wasteland science!"

Pinot remembered Clem too well. The leading med at the clinic, she'd worked closely with them the last time she'd visited Summerland. Clem would probably tell the whole town, *the healer has returned!* She'd have to make this quick.

"Clem?" she interrupted the med's ongoing dissertation. "I think you have me confused with someone—"

"Oh!" Clem exclaimed and slapped their forehead. "I should give you some tetanus boosters to take back to the Restaurant!"

Pinot winced. "Can't. I haven't been there for a while."

"Sorry to hear that," Clem said. "Is everything okay?"

"Yeah." Pinot disembarked from the high stool, the floor unsteady as she took a step toward the door. "I should head—"

Clem was beside her, a gentle hand supporting her elbow. "By the way, I ran out of the stuff you left last time," they said. "You don't have any more of those homemade pills, do you? We're really hurting for extra supplies since the Pacific line got cut."

"What's that?" Pinot stopped, suddenly alert.

"We had a medical contact in one of the coastal communities out west. An old bottling factory, ran basic meds to Summerland since Year 3. But it's been quiet since the spring. Not a trader, Grafter, or otherwise coming from that way in a king's age."

Something shifted in Pinot's gut. She didn't know why the news made her uncomfortable, but she knew the feeling: something bad on the horizon. "I'll see what I can do, just…" Pinot released a breath. "Promise you won't tell anyone else I'm here? They'll swarm me like a free buffet."

"Not my fault you have a reputation in this town," Clem grinned. "Cross my heart. Drop by anytime, you know where I'll be!"

Pinot waved to Caden across the room and motioned to the door. He nodded, and she left, walking the cold road home.

***

It felt like she'd just fallen asleep when Pinot heard voices. Probably just Jeff and Caden coming back from the Juice Bar. She turned over, ignoring the loud words, someone calling her name—

"Pinot! Wake up, hey!"

Shaking her shoulder, insistent. Someone in her room? Pinot jumped awake grasping for the switchblade that wasn't there.

"It's Clem, it's me. We need you, we need you, okay?" Clem stood up with a grunt, pushing the tarp in the doorway aside. "Please, hurry."

Pinot unclenched her hands and pulled on her hiking boots. She'd fallen asleep in her clothes, but her whole body shivered as she grabbed her gloves and her canteen. The sense of foreboding that had started at the Juice Bar swelled as she followed Clem outside.

"Are Jeff and Caden okay?" Pinot said, jogging to keep up with Clem's all-business pace.

"Yes, oh sorry, of course you'd think that! They're just getting the extra beds out of storage."

"What—?" Pinot's throat closed. Her entire body froze. Clustered outside of the clinic was a group of people in white shorts and t-shirts with delicate silver rings arching up over their shoulders. "Fuck. No." She ran to them, names and faces she hadn't thought of in years crowding in on her. The people around her were starved, bruised, barely able to stand. "Where is he?" she asked them, but they stared at her with huge empty eyes.

"Let us through, please." Clem led Pinot into the clinic. Turning right in the cramped entryway, they went through to the infirmary side of the low building. A handful of the people were already laid out on cots along the side wall.

"Help them." Clem handed her a blue apron and a pair of latex gloves. "All the supplies are in the cabinet by the desk. Al?" Clem called the other med over. "Bring them all inside, we'll have to use mats until Caden and Jeff get the extra beds set up."

Dazed, Pinot put on the apron and moved to the closest patient. Not allowing herself to recognize them, she checked vitals, looked for signs of illness, got them to drink a bit of spit-spiked water from her canteen. Then the next patient, and then the next.

"You…" one said, lifting a bone-and-sinew arm from the mat. "I know you…"

"Just relax," Pinot said, helping them drink. "You're safe here."

Jeff and Caden brought in extra beds. Pinot moved a penlight over a dilated pupil trying not to see the face it was set in. Clem moved from patient to patient, smiling reassurance and making sure everyone was comfortable.

Finally, all twenty-two of the group had a place to recover. Leaving Al in charge of the infirmary, Clem and Pinot headed to the research side of the clinic. In silence, Clem took a large ring of keys from their pocket and flipped through them. Unlocking the door, they led Pinot inside.

Clem pulled aside a curtain to reveal a simple medical workshop set with a chair, a bench, a tiny refrigerator unit, and a table of supplies.

"Jesus-fucking-Christ," Clem finally said, sinking onto the bench.

Pinot took off her apron.

Clem's usually cheery demeanour had completely fallen away, leaving them sombre, unfamiliar. They pushed the wild hair up from their forehead, their eyes staring into the far corner of the room. "Malnourished, dehydrated, some with bedsores—what the hell does it mean? And all dressed the same. Some kind of cult?"

"No," Pinot said. "Not a cult."

"And the metal over their shoulders, attached to the ribs on the front and back with medical tape. Someone conducting experiments, maybe. For what purpose?"

Pinot took the chair across from Clem. "I know who they are." She tightly wrapped the apron in her hands, trying to avoid Clem's expectant gaze. "I used to call them Partiers, but they're more like scientists. They live in machines called Survival Units. Cross the wasteland. Led by, uh," she swallowed, "someone named Jax. But he's not with them."

"What does that mean?" Clem asked quietly. "They escaped?"

Pinot gripped the blue fabric in her hands, trying to forget the host of starved faces. Had Jax done that?

Maybe there was still time. She ran out of the research room, whipping the apron against the wall as she burst out of the clinic.

She didn't stop running until she was outside of the settlement, facing the black wasteland under the dark grey of a cloud-swathed night. She scanned the horizon for the glow of one hundred eyes, a bronze sheen in the distance. There was nothing.

Chapter 19
Pinot and Jax
in the Past

Five years previous, the wasteland

Pinot heard the truck bed groan, felt through waking how it tilted underneath her. Someone had boarded her sleeping place. She opened one eye, finding the figure through the cross-hatch openings in the crate wall. She gripped the switchblade in her pocket.

The blot on the night sky approached and then stopped, sat down on the metal floor. "Hey, Millerite. You awake?" Jax's voice.

She took her hands from her pockets. "What's up, Opaldine?"

"Couldn't sleep."

Pinot crawled out from her crate fort, settling warily across from him. "You thinking of Keats?"

Jax didn't reply, but she noticed him tense up. It wasn't something she could see—more of a change in the air.

"You were pretty close, huh?" Her words settled into the space between them.

"Yeah. He…he didn't take my bullshit, you know?"

Pinot thought back to a couple days before, standing outside of a domed Survival Unit while Jax tried to reason with Keats. *She can heal you…The Event gave her abilities, I know it sounds crazy…*

Please Keats… The sick Partier had refused to come out. "Sorry I couldn't help him."

The shadow of Jax's hands scuffed up his mohawk. "It's not like you didn't try. They just… they're scared of anything from the outside. Even if it can help."

"It's like being a Millerite or an Opaldine, isn't it? Everybody outside the gang is out to get you."

Jax drew his boots along the truck bed until his knees were bent up, blending into the shadow of his chest. "More people are going to die."

Pinot imagined May and Isak asleep in the cab of the truck, Ed wandering through the Partiers. A picture of Jax's dead body in the wasteland flashed through her mind. "Where are we going, Jax?"

Something like a laugh and then, quietly, "I want to see if the ocean is still there."

"The ocean?"

"Everything else, it's gone. But the sea? Have you seen it, how it just goes on forever? It's the best at night, like a black sheet of glass, blacker than the sky even. This—" he motioned up, "—it looks dark, but it's not. Not really."

"I've never been."

"We'll get there eventually. Then you can see it. If you want to."

Pinot scoffed, crossing her arms. "I have a choice now?"

"You can go whenever you want. The rest of them, too. When I made you leave the convenience store, I thought I was neutralising a potential threat. But I think I can trust you now. You can go, anytime. I'm not going to stop you."

Pinot weighed the sincerity of his words, trying to make out his grey features. "The sea, huh?"

"If it's still there." The shadow of his hand reached out toward her and hung between them, a faint outline.

After a moment, Pinot lifted her hand. The shadows of their hands merged in the warm darkness.

Chapter 20
Isak and Sophie Play Cards

By the time winter arrived, Isak was settled into his new routine at the restaurant. People got used to him bunking in the dorm and stopped asking him how he was. It was understood that he and May were taking some kind of break. May stopped wearing her wedding rings and kept Arissa or Victoria near her whenever Isak was around as a kind of buffer. Isak spent more and more time with Nick and Sophie.

Once a day, he'd join Sophie for cards or team up with her to do the laundry or some other chore. Sophie did a lot of things around the restaurant, more than Isak was ever aware of. She shook out the mats in the entryways and organised the books and games in the downstairs sitting area. She took compost to the fenced-in bin a couple metres into the woods and managed the weekly generator-usage schedule. She cut people's hair. She took around a sign-up list for Catherine's ASL class and the interviews Rhonda was doing for the archive. She taught Stef and Markus how to sew. On kitchen duty, she cooked up simple, hearty dishes with the minimal ingredients the restaurant had on hand. Isak had thought her dampening ability was impressive, but her social and productive days showed her true power.

Isak rarely jumped through time anymore. The tasks he and Sophie worked on together kept him in the moment and his mind occupied. When he had free time, he went to the sitting area to read, the sunset illuminating the room with a rich orange glow. If it wasn't for his break-up with May, he would've felt content.

May tried to make it easier on him. She would leave him and Lucas alone when they played cars in the bedroom or went on ambling adventures through the restaurant. Lucas was starting to take small, wavering steps, and he called Isak by name. Sometimes, Isak joined May at the dining room table to help feed Lucas pieces of boiled vegetables and broth. Isak would hold Lucas and May would turn away without comment. Slowly, it started to feel normal.

***

Isak sat down at the dining hall table as Sophie laid out a game of Kings in the Corner, one of her favourites. They both picked up their hands and silently began the game. Their daily meetings were a balm for Isak—there was never pressure to talk. They could play a whole game without saying anything beyond commenting on the cards or the need to make tea when the game was done. But today, Isak had a question.

"I was wondering," Isak said once Sophie had drawn a card.

"Oh yes?" Sophie studied the series of cards around the draw pile.

"When May and I were at the cabin, I didn't jump as much. That was you, wasn't it?"

Sophie winked one of her walnut-lidded eyes at him. "Old women can still go on walks through the forest, can't they?" She finished a row and collected the cards into a neat stack.

"I know that May thinks you were doing something wrong, but I appreciate you looking out for me."

Sophie chuckled. "I'm used to it."

"Do you…did you have kids?" Isak said, hearing something else under her words.

Sophie lowered her cards, tapping a crooked finger on the table. "I had six younger brothers." Her blue eyes took on a thoughtful look. "My parents died, you see, so it was my responsibility to watch over them. Oh, how I wanted to be like those happy young women I saw in the movies, so free of responsibility, going on dates and wearing pretty clothes." Sophie clucked her tongue. "But that wasn't for me. At the time, it seemed to go on forever. But looking back, it wasn't that long at all. I learned so many things that kept me going later on in life." She crossed one hand over the other on the table. "I'm used to watching over people, just like I used to look out for my brothers. I miss them. More than anything."

"I'm sorry," Isak said as Sophie picked up her cards and returned her attention to the game.

"It's in the past," Sophie said, matter-of-fact. "They all had good lives, and I'm very proud of them." She smiled at Isak. "It's your turn."

Log Entry 16:

Jax destroyed a facility in the wasteland. Got out of his S.U. and laughed at the people coming out of the concrete jail to meet him with guns. The weapon went off—a timer or remote setting?—taking out half of the building in one hit.

One heat reading on my screen moved away from the building—one survivor.

I hacked into his S.U. from my own and erased that one reading. Will he find out? I can't keep my hands from shaking.

But I have one bright spot of hope: I saved a life. There's one person out there that he didn't get.

Book Two
Year 7

Chapter 1
Rhonda Interviews

"Where should I…?" Isak asked as Rhonda moved further into Ed's office.

"Oh, there's a chair there for you."

"Thanks." Isak sat down and scooted up to the round table Rhonda had brought from the dining hall. "So, I'm your first one?"

"Yes," Rhonda said, taking a clipboard from the metal shelf and trying to hold it in a way that didn't make her feel like a psychologist in a first-year film project. "I'm looking forward to hearing whatever you want to tell me."

"For the archive, right? Do you have questions, or should I just dive in?"

Rhonda settled into the padded wheely chair on the other side of the table. "Oh, it's casual, you can tell me and I'll take notes, or you can write down whatever."

"I was thinking about telling you—"

Rhonda blinked, momentarily startled at Isak's sudden disappearance. "This is normal," she reminded herself. She titled the page secured to the clipboard, wondering how long she should wait.

A minute later, Isak blipped into being. "Sorry," he apologised from the chair, a full glass of water in his hand. "I was really thirsty." He took a deep drink and set it down.

"Definitely ready now."

"I thought Sophie was helping with your time travelling?" Rhonda said, her curiosity getting in the way of her interview schedule.

"She's been isolating in the clinic for a few days now. Bronchitis again."

"And the dampening, or whatever, doesn't work if she's not around."

"Yeah." Isak drained the glass of water. "Okay. Should I start?"

"Go ahead."

There was a knock and the door opened just enough for Nick to poke his head in. "Sorry to interrupt, but May can't find Lucas's bottle—"

"Oh," Isak half-stood, "I left it near the—you know what, I'll just get it. Be right back," Isak apologised and followed Nick out of the office. "She could've just asked me…" Footsteps on the stairs shook the metal shelving unit on the wall.

Left alone, Rhonda scanned the office. She'd rearranged the room to make it more "interview-y", with the table in the middle of the closet-sized space, but there were no windows and the room was featureless, too separate from the rest of the restaurant. In a movie, she'd be conducting interrogations in this tiny, fluorescent-lit room—all it needed was a swinging lightbulb, styrofoam cups of coffee, and a cigarette in an ashtray.

She should plan to hold future interviews somewhere else— in the dining area, maybe, or in the gaming room when no one else was around. At least there'd be windows, a place to look when the interview went too deep or got too sad. She was asking people to talk about the end of the world, after all.

Light thumping on the stairs, one set of feet, a slight metallic hum from the shelving unit.

"He's going to be a minute." Nick came in and settled across from her. "Not the start you were hoping for?"

Rhonda shook her head. "It's okay. I'm still figuring it out."

Nick opened a hand on the wood-grain table. "It's the

middle of winter, there's not much else to do. You can take your time."

Rhonda took his hand. "You didn't sign up."

He squeezed and let go. "Half the restaurant's on there already. Even Catherine! That'll be something worth adding to the archive!"

Rhonda doodled on the clipboard paper. "You don't talk about your life before very much."

Nick half-lifted a hand to his hair, then crossed his arms instead. "Not much to tell. Nothing that would come close to what everyone else has gone through."

Rhonda waited for him to continue. When he didn't, she set the clipboard aside. "If you want to tell me, outside of the archive, I'm listening."

"Maybe one day." Nick got up and swung his arms back and across his chest as if he was warming up for a run. "I feel like tea, want some?"

"Nick?" Rhonda waited until he turned back from the door and then signed 'I love you.'

He crossed the room, held her face in both of his hands. They kissed.

The shelving unit vibrated against the wall as someone came down the stairs. Nick moved away and Rhonda melted into the padded chair, her whole body warm.

"He's back," Nick said as Isak came into the room.

"Sorry about that." Isak tucked a stray piece of hair behind his ear. "No more interruptions!"

Rhonda caught sight of Nick in the doorway. 'I love you,' he signed. He closed the door behind him.

Taking a deep breath to settle her racing heart, Rhonda picked up her clipboard. "Okay, Isak. Tell me what life was like, after the end."

Isak sat back in his chair and began. "May and I used to live in a house on what used to be Holly Street…"

Chapter 2
Pinot Gets Another Lead

Pinot side-stepped around the weighted tarp over the door to the Phone Book.

"I was waiting for you!" Lorraine said, wheeling out from around the desk.

"Am I late?" Pinot held a thermos of tea in one hand, her canteen in the other. A weekly tradition that had grown out of Pinot's regular check-ins on her inquiry.

"This isn't about the tea!" Lorraine paused, then took the chipped thermos in her mittened hands. "Well, yes, thank you, I am excited for a hot drink. But that's not it!" She led Pinot to the low table. When they were both settled, Lorraine took an index card from her pocket.

"Is that it?" Pinot said, feeling a knot deep in her stomach. "Did someone see Ed?"

Lorraine nodded. "Did you hear about the traveller who came into town last week?"

"I thought it was a rumour. It's too cold for anyone to be out on the wasteland this time of year."

"Well, I can't explain it, but she's at the clinic. She asked for me. Wanted to see if I'd heard about her family. In exchange, she gave me information…"

"Is it bad?" Pinot asked when Lorraine didn't continue.

"There were at least fifteen where she was, but probably

more, she said. And one of them was Ed. Same description."

Pinot gripped her knees. "What happened?"

"She wouldn't say."

"What's her name?"

"Fayette. But no one's supposed to...."

Pinot didn't hear the rest. She crossed the room in a daze, went out into the town courtyard. The cold didn't register as she made her way across the packed snow.

The clinic was exactly as she remembered from the night the Partiers arrived. Two main rooms joined by a narrow entryway, most of it taken up by a fold-out table covered in handwritten brochures on everything from tetanus to oral hygiene. A med she didn't recognize noticed her through the open door to the infirmary.

"Do you need help?" they asked, wiping their hands on a towel.

"Me?" Pinot said, keeping her voice gruff, to the point. "Is there a Fayette here?"

The med frowned, bracing their arm on the doorframe. "Lorraine told you? She should know better. Fayette deserves to be left alone."

Clem popped their round face between the doorway and the med's arm. "Oh hey Pinot, thought I heard your voice!"

The med's mouth dropped open.

"That's her, alright, the healer in the flesh," Clem grinned up at their colleague. "Come on in," they waved Pinot into the infirmary, leaving the other med speechless at the door.

"Who's that?" Pinot asked as Clem went over to the cabinet.

"Oh, Shiloh? She's from the resident sector, wants to get out of agriculture and into medicine! Promising so far—"

"Clem," Pinot interrupted. "I gotta see Fayette."

"Oh!" Clem seemed surprised. "But I thought you were here to make a generous donation?" They gave Pinot a pointed look. "You've been avoiding me all month."

"Where's Fayette?" Pinot said, trying to keep her visit on track.

"Oh yeah, well, she's asleep right now. Got her on sleeping teas. You know, we've been trying out herbal teas for boosting the immune system—"

"When can I talk to her?"

"Should wear off in a half hour or so. We could try some of your healing stuff, that's an idea, though I'm not sure if that would help anything. Seemed best to let her stay here until—"

"Okay," Pinot said, moving to the door. "Let's get this over with."

"Here." Clem handed Pinot a mason jar and a loop of surgical tubing.

"Yeah, yeah, take my blood, sweat, and tears, whatever you need," Pinot sighed as she followed Clem to the research side of the clinic.

"I meant to ask," Clem said over their shoulder as they unlocked the door. "It's pretty clear that you don't want to be involved here. When did you stop practising?"

"What?"

"Practising medicine."

Pinot followed them into the research room. "Magical healing powers, remember? I was only playing at being a doctor."

Clem grew serious. "You helped a lot of people. That's what a doctor's supposed to do. You lived up to it. At least, you did for us."

Pinot let the comment pass. She placed the jar and tubing on the supply table.

All business, Clem handed her a tiny square of cotton on a toothpick. "Swab, please."

Pinot wiped the inside of her cheek with it, grimacing at the texture. Next, they gave her the mason jar to spit in. Then, Clem tied a piece of rubber tubing around her upper arm and drew a vial of blood. Pinot felt a shiver go through her as she watched the blood fill the chamber. The last time someone had taken blood from her, it had been a far more intimate affair.

"Perfect! I'll get these put away nice and safe here…" Clem placed the samples in a sealed tupperware container, wrote a messy label that Pinot could not make out and secreted them into the small refrigerator.

"Is Jessie still doing that soil breakdown?" Pinot asked as Clem handed her a cup of grape juice.

"Trying to figure out what happened? Yeah. It's pretty wild, considering xe's been on it almost three years and has nothing conclusive. There should definitely be some indication of what caused the Event, some trace. But nada. Just a severe lack of biological matter in the topsoil, at least from the first samples. Been building up since then."

"Still think it could've been something chemical?"

Settling against the wall, Clem gazed up at the ceiling. "Maybe we're in an alternate universe, like some have theorised. Pushed just out of phase with regular space-time by a solar flare or a black hole echo. Who knows? Even with Jessie's studies, it could be decades before we can be sure of anything. In the meantime, I'm going to try and keep as many of us alive as possible."

Pinot swirled the juice, the strong smell of vineyards rising up to her. "How are the Partiers doing?"

"Still recovering at the inn. Mostly just trying to get them on a steady diet." Clem shook their head, their wild grey and brown hair taking a moment longer to stop moving. "It's a miracle they survived. You know it was some kind of hibernation setting in their Survival Units? Weeks and months at a time. The body isn't meant to endure that."

"I'm just glad they got out."

Clem checked their watch. "You're good to go," they told her. "If you feel faint from the blood sample, let me know. Fayette's in the far bed with the blue curtain around it."

Pinot drained the juice dregs and set the cup on the workbench. "Anything I should know?"

"Oof, yeah, Fayettee is...uh, not doing great, to be honest. Another miracle there. Came through winter on the wasteland without a hint of frostbite—physically, she's alright. But she's been through a lot. Can you promise you'll leave if she starts to get agitated?"

"'Course."

Pinot closed the research area door behind her. Her eyes caught on the gauze bandage Clem had applied to the needle mark. As she went into the infirmary, she unwrapped it, satisfied to see that her skin had already covered the dot of blood.

Pinot approached the far bed, gently pulling the curtain aside. "Fayette?" she asked.

The patient turned her head, matching Pinot's eyes with a distant grey stare. Her gold hair was cut in a short wave, her white skin blanched further by fatigue. Blue and red veins stood out across her bare arms.

Fayette's eyes narrowed. "Who are you?"

"Nobody you have to worry about," Pinot said softly, sitting on a chair next to the cot. "Just wanted to ask you a question."

Fayette didn't reply, keeping her eyes on Pinot.

"Do you know...I'm looking for my friend. He was taken away a while ago, but I heard you may have seen him recently. His name's Ed."

Fayette drew in a sharp breath, her hands twisting the blanket covering her. "You know him?"

"I'm Pinot, and—"

"Pinot!" Fayette said, a spark catching in her eyes. "Of course! Ed told me all about you!"

"He did?" Pinot said doubtfully.

"We didn't have pens and paper," Fayette explained, "but he'd trace out words on the ground, or on my hand—" She broke off suddenly, covering her eyes.

"Where can I find him?" Pinot asked after a moment. "I want to help him."

"I'm going to have a baby," Fayette whispered.

Pinot felt the dread in Fayette's announcement, and leaned closer, trying to show support for whatever she might say next.

Fayette swallowed and lowered her hands. "The facility didn't just study us," she said, her voice shaking. "They...they wanted to make more. More people with powers. An army."

"Ed's ability to control electricity..." Pinot could see how people might want to take advantage of a power like that.

Fayette nodded. "I can change the weather around me, and I always know which way is north," she said. "They took me from the camp I lived in with my family..."

When Fayette didn't continue, Pinot picked up on her earlier thought. "The baby was somehow part of their plan, to make an army?"

Fayette wiped her eyes. "They kept us in pairs, you know. Locked up in cells. They put things in our food, drugs maybe? Hormones? Ed and I...He never did anything unless I asked him to...but after I got pregnant, we were separated. I never saw him after that."

Pinot pushed down the rage that threatened to consume her. Instead, she focused on Fayette. "How did you escape?"

"One night, I woke up and the door to my room was open. There was a sound, a huge explosion, fire everywhere. I ran, found the back exit, just kept running..." Fayette stopped, her eyes going blank.

"And eventually you made it here," Pinot finished for her.

Fayette smoothed the blanket over her stomach.

"Can you tell me where this facility is?"

"Due southwest of here. Two days of walking. Please, if you go..." Fayette swallowed. "Be careful. They have powers of their own, ways to block your ability and trap you."

"You don't have to worry about me," Pinot smiled.

"Ed told me about you. You were very dear to him..."

Pinot placed her hand on Fayette's shoulder. "I'm sorry." It was all she could say.

Fayette turned away from her. Pinot got up from the chair and left the clinic.

She reached the tenement neighbourhood and sheltered behind the tea hut, lighting the last of Lily's cigarettes. She took a deep draw, trying to focus on the taste, the smell, not the rage, not the guilt. The end of the cigarette burned and fell away, ashes hissing in the snow around her boots.

Someone emerged from between the shacks, carrying a bowl of water. Battered duster jacket, broad shoulders. Jeff.

Noticing Pinot, he looked up from the bowl, his face clean-shaven.

"You shave?" Pinot said.

Jeff chuckled, tossing the beard-flecked water from the bowl onto the road. "Once a year, just so I don't forget what it feels like."

"But your chin is going to get cold."

Jeff shrugged. "My chin can handle it."

Pinot took another draw from the cigarette. She offered it to Jeff, but he held up a hand, leaning on the corrugated metal wall of the shack across from her. "What's going on?" he asked after a moment. "You look upset."

Pinot shook her head. "I know where Ed is. Or was."

"Holy shit! That's huge. Is he okay?"

"I don't know."

Jeff followed her gaze past the tenement sector, out towards the snow-covered wasteland. "How far?"

"Two days."

"You can't go," Jeff said. "It's too cold. Not until spring."

"I know." Pinot's tears spilled over, leaving prickly lines on her cheeks.

Log Entry 21:

We haven't been moving as much. Long stretches of time in one place. Is Jax using the time to improve the weapon, to plan his next move? He must've made contact with one of the defunct satellites, it's the only way he could pinpoint these random locations on the wasteland.

But I've been busy, too. Since the others escaped, Jax hasn't implemented the hibernation setting. Does he trust me or just think one lone scientist is easier to control? Is he watching me?

So far, my minor hacks into my S.U. haven't drawn his attention. I think if push came to shove, I could hack his hatch controls, but navigation and weapon control are completely inaccessible from here. Even taking control of all the other S.U.s would be risky. Keeping the data safe has to come first.

Eventually, he'll have to ask my advice on something, give me access—I'm the last person he has, the last scientist. Why else would he keep me alive?

Chapter 3
Isak and the Gift

Catherine and Ksenia taught an ASL class on Wednesday evenings. Isak sat with Nick and Rhonda, trying to copy the signs Catherine demonstrated with fluid and graceful movements. Ksenia explained the signs and showed examples of her own staccato versions. She reminded Isak of Pinot at that age, a teenager on the edge of adulthood, clearly resenting being forced to engage with the other residents. He tried his best to follow her brief instructions, watching Catherine to make sure he was using the correct hand for the correct movement.

Nick and Rhonda were already comfortable with signing and joked with each other between learning new phrases. After the class, Nick went up to Catherine and signed what Isak thought was 'thank you' and 'I like your hair'. Catherine replied, something too fast for Isak to read. Rhonda joined Nick next to the fireplace, and the two of them left holding hands. Ksenia stomped downstairs as Catherine sat with Arissa, a mug of tea ready and waiting for her.

The rest of the residents thinned out, heading off to bed or other quiet evening activities. On the far side of the dining hall, May sat with Lucas propped up on her knee, studying the notes she'd taken down on the back of an old phone book.

Isak tapped the tin in his jeans pocket for good luck. He made his way over to May. "Hi," he waved, continuing to sign as he asked, "how are you?"

"Good," May signed. She dropped her hands to hold Lucas more securely on her knee.

"Can I sit with you?" he asked. "It won't take long."

"Sure," she said, trying to keep a light smile on her face.

Isak sat down and took the tin out of his pocket. It was dented, an old case for protractors and rulers, a little mathematics kit for a student. He cleared his throat. "I made something for you." Isak placed the tin within her reach.

May paused, then flipped the lid open. The inside of the tin had been segmented into one-inch squares. Each contained a different colour of coarse powder.

"Sophie taught me how to make them." Isak clenched his hand under the table. "I hope you like it."

"Are these—" May's voice caught and she paused to take a breath. "Are these pigments?"

"Yes," Isak swallowed. "They're made of natural materials. And I even—" He scrambled to take the pocket-sized paintbrush out of his coat and set it next to the tin. "I thought that when I'm looking after Lucas you could get back into painting. If you want."

Tears pooled in May's eyes. "Isak…"

"It's a gift, between friends." He smiled weakly. "Whatever happens…I'd like to be friends, still. If that's okay with you."

May frowned, Lucas starting to fidget in her arms. She lowered him to the floor, then raised her eyes back to the paint tin. "Yes," she said with something like relief. "I'd like that."

A rush went through Isak. "Really?"

"Yes," May met his eyes, hopeful, lonely, content. "Still friends."

Archive Interview #9
Location: Ulway's Restaurant and Retreat Centre
Medium: Handwritten by interviewee

Catherine's Account of the Event, Lantern, and Reaching the Forest

The school wanted to hold Ksenia back a year. That's what Reid and I talked about during the night-drive on the highway, Ksenia already asleep in the backseat. More that I talked, I guess—he gave little nods or one-handed responses, one eye on the road, always. A normal thing to talk about, a normal night, driving our sleeping kid home from summer camp. She'd liked it, the outdoor life, full of easy activities and not a lot asked of her. School was different. There were tests she didn't pass, and the other kids called her a baby when she cried, considering themselves so mature, sixth graders at the top of the school food chain. Ksenia wasn't there yet, the teachers said. She'd need special classes to keep up, some extra help.

Reid thought it much ado about nothing. For him, grade school was extended daycare. Who cared if her grades were low, this wasn't college.

But it adds up, I argued. If she can't keep up now, better for her to have extra time, get used to it.

She's not stupid, Reid signed, then gripped the wheel, turning both eyes away.

I watched the highway signs pass for a while.

Pull over, I told him. There's something weird.

Weird? he asked, but pulled over without hesitation.

Like a bad storm or a tornado, I said, something in the air.

He engaged the emergency brake, fidgeted with the radio knob.

The ground underneath the car hummed then rattled—I felt it jar up my feet, all through the body of the car.

Ksenia woke up and tapped my shoulder. What's happening? she asked.

I gripped her hand, to reassure her, reassure myself.

The earthquake heaved under us. The world outside was dark. Ksenia's sleeping bag, hordes of driving snacks, car debris jumbled around us as the car bucked up from the earth. Chaos, until it was over.

We set everything to rights. Reid frowned at the radio. It's not picking up anything, he said.

But the car started up again fine and Reid drove slowly, testing the brakes and the acceleration. It's okay, he said.

The smooth highway gave way to dirt. Did we take a wrong turn? I asked.

We backtracked, found the pavement. Drove in that direction until the road disappeared again.

What the hell? Reid's mouth said, a fist on the steering wheel.

We drove up and down that piece of highway until I said we should wait for someone to come rescue us. That's what you did if there was an earthquake or flood, if you got lost in the woods.

You know what it was like. Right after it happened. When the world didn't make sense. Had to make sure it was really gone. And then. What else was there to do?

Our first night sleeping in the car. The next day, we drove in the direction that was supposed to lead home, but ended up leading nowhere. We lived out of the car, eating snacks, finding little places along the way, taking what we could. Sometimes we drove past knotted groups of ragged people, who would chase us until we left them in the dust.

Our fuel ran out. We lived out of our car until we ran out of food. We walked. After a long time of living on the wasteland, a ragged group found us. Reid tried to fight them off, but they were quick with their killing. When they started eating him, I grabbed Ksenia's hand and ran. We ran and walked and slept and ran.

We came upon a tall fence. Someone came out to bring us in, a mother and child. We were so weak with hunger and exhaustion. They didn't ask us any questions. Gave us food and a place to wash and new clothes. Ksenia kept running her hand over the handmade dress in wonder. When was the last time we'd been so clean? Years?

We lived there, at the compound. A farm commune. A cult. Call it any of those things. They called it Lantern, their shining light in the corruption of the wasteland.

After a while, they asked if I was married. Widowed, I said— some of them knew ASL, and for the rest, I carried a chalkboard tablet around. You must remarry, one said, it's our way here.

I thought of Ksenia and agreed. There was a celebration for the marriage. The man was cruel-hearted, but I endured it for Ksenia's sake. Compared to the wasteland, it was heaven.

Once they reached 13, children no longer lived with their parents. They slept in a separate dorm, went to worship services, helped in the fields, and eventually took on an apprenticeship. Ksenia did well at spinning and dyeing wool. She loved it there. I cried to see her so happy. I protected her with my silence.

I broke, only once. Couldn't take it. Ran away. Didn't get far. The wasteland frightened me too much. I went back.

And I was punished. Leaving the compound, abandoning my child. I was an evil woman.

They took me to the worship house, where every morning we sang songs and gave offerings to their god. Just the men. My husband watched as they stripped me down to my underclothes and took turns branding me with rods they heated in the holy candles of the place. Not on my face or hands. I still must seem whole for the children, who were kept ignorant of adults and their terrible rules.

I submitted to those rules. For my own sake now, as well as Ksenia's. I'd been reminded of the horrors out on the wasteland. At least inside the compound there was food, shelter, the quiet company of the other women, some of them proud, some of them shamed like me. I was ashamed of my body after that. Ashamed of being a woman. I hid among them, another set of hands to help take care of the constant stream of babies, another demure face bowed in prayer. Secretly, I thanked God that I never had another child.

Ksenia loved Lantern. She loved the fields, the animals, and her friends. Eventually, I became nothing more than a shadow to her. A reminder of the terrible world she passed through to reach home.

But she was about to turn 18. At 18, young women were married off. That was their way. Everyone knew that one of the elders who ran the compound wanted to make Ksenia his bride. He was 56, and had already been married twice. He had several children. Both of his wives died giving birth.

I had to get Ksenia out of there. I should've gotten her out long before. It was the idea of her married to a cruel man, trapped and beaten-down like I was, that spurred me into action. I didn't eat for days, putting aside all the food I could. I stuffed it in a pillowcase, handspun like everything else in the compound, waited for the last moonless night before Ksenia's wedding. She didn't know. She wouldn't be told until the night before, when she'd be pampered and dressed in a fine white dress to await the morning, the celebration, the first night of despair.

I asked her to come over for dinner. I said, let's go for a walk. I had the pillowcase of food tied under my skirt. There was a weak place in the fence by the sheep pen, and I pushed her through it. Maybe she yelled for help, but it was empty in the fields at night, and I didn't let go of her hand. I pulled her into the wasteland, away from the place she considered home. She never forgave me. But I don't care. I got us out of there.

We walked north, north, north. For days and days. We finished all of our food. Ksenia wanted to go back. She promised she'd be good. She said I was a bad woman and if I took her home she'd forgive me. The wasteland frightened her too much to even think about going back alone.

The trading caravan found us a couple days later. I asked to travel with them, and they agreed. A woman and her child. We were to be pitied.

I wept when we reached the forest. I'd believed that the compound was all the life left in the world. In spite of everything, I felt ashamed of leaving it. But the trees and the earth and the flowers, alive and well and untamed—I can't express how much it moved me. The world is still alive, I cried to myself. I am still alive. That is the only lesson. That's the way to keep living.

Chapter 4
Pinot in the
Wasteland

Covered in soft mounds of snow, with puddles dotting it like mirrors, the wasteland was different from what Pinot remembered from her early days of post-apocalyptic travel. Back then, it was a grey field of playdough, dull and bare, completely clear of vegetation. But over the past few years, plant life started spreading over the surface of the wasteland as if licking up an oil spill—grasses and moss and ivy and ferns fanned out from the patches of life that remained like islands in the barren landscape. Vegetation spread with a stunning alacrity, building up soil and nutrients for larger flowers and plants.

Walking through the wasteland now was like crossing an area of tundra, everything sparse and spare, but alive. Like a great glacier, the Event had swept the rest away, leaving the path behind it ripe for a new beginning. Even though the wind was cutting and the sun was still too-bright, the smell of spring was undeniable: growth, water, and crisp air full of possibility. The scent was heady and fresh. It made her hungry.

Pinot ate through the raisins that Jeff and Caden had given her, keeping her canteen as a last resort for when the hunger got bad. It would take a couple days of walking to get to the facility, Fayette had said. The ground was soft and the slush slippery. It was hard to get a fire going, even though she'd brought a bag of firewood and slow-burning moss along.

Pinot squinted through the slits in the fabric wrapped over her eyes—another gift from Jeff, who knew what early spring was like on the wasteland. The fabric dulled the effect of the sun's full force reflecting off the melting snow in a searing white-hot feast of light. After the winter of staying mostly indoors, full sunlight was unbearable.

She took the compass from inside her jacket, let her eyes adjust as she studied the dashes on the clear plastic surface. She was still on course. One more day until she reached the facility, if she believed Fayette's story. But why would Fayette lie? She had definitely seen Ed, knew things about him. But if there was a fire at the facility, did that mean...?

Pinot tucked the compass away, readjusted her backpack. She had to keep moving—she was wearing all of her clothes, but the cold was starting to make her bare fingers ache. Ahead of her, miles of gleaming and melting wasteland. Beyond that? Somewhere unseen, a facility, answers. The cold blue sky over all.

***

The facility was decimated. Ruined walls and blackened chunks of concrete were piled about like surreal pyramids. Did some of them cover bodies? Was Ed one of them?

Pinot shook the thought from her mind, following what looked to be a walkway under all of the rubble. A crow cawed three times from somewhere in the ruins and an echoing cry responded from the wasteland. Were they warning of a human intruder, unsure if she was friend or foe?

You don't need to worry about me, Pinot thought to the crows, *I'm just passing through.*

She picked her way over seared drywall and melted spots of metal draped over concrete debris. If she could believe what Fayette had told her, the place had been burned two months ago. It reminded her of a hospital ward.

A surprisingly intact marble welcome desk waited for her in the middle of the ruin. Heat from the fire had done away with any papers and the computer had been smashed. Doorways branched off, some just openings in the half-burned down wall. Pinot picked her way through the rooms, finding bars in the windows and electromagnetic locks on the heavy metal doors that lay angled on the ground. Not a hospital, then. A prison.

Pinot returned to the welcome desk and searched for answers. She pulled out the drawers, finding nothing but ashes, splatters of plastic and metal. The lock on the drawer under the marble surface of the desk had completely melted away. She opened it and immediately closed her eyes. There was something in the drawer that she recognized.

Up until now, there had been the possibility that Fayette was lying. That Ed hadn't been taken to this terrible place to be drugged and used and discarded. But the evidence was there, if she had the courage to see it. She forced herself to look in the drawer. To pick up the switchblade, the handle twisted, the closed blade fused inside of it. It was the knife she had given to Ed just before he disappeared.

She pocketed the useless blade and grimly returned to the prison entrance. She circled the outside of the facility, looking for footprints, anything.

Something stopped her cold. There were deep tracks in the ground leading away from the facility, visible even after two months of weather. They were as wide as a house, as even as a shovelled path cut through snow. She recognized them. She feared them.

A crow cawed as it took flight from the rubble.

The tracks were made by a horde of Survival Units. Twenty or so, their trails large enough to be mistaken for wind grooves on the wasteland. Had Jax used the SUs to burn down the facility? Or had he come through after the fact and cleaned out the place? Scavenged what he could for the SUs all-accepting power converters, all the papers she needed, the information lost, ground into bone meal for their systems? Pinot lined up her compass's wavering needle with the wide tracks. The SUs were headed east.

She cast back in her memory, trying to pull up everything

she knew about the Survival Units. Did they have weapons? She'd never been inside of one—when she'd travelled with them, the SUs kept to themselves, speaking in code, shunning the wasteland air. As an outsider, Pinot hadn't made many friends among them. Only Eliot. And Jax.

Suddenly, she was 17 years old again and in love with him. A volatile relationship, built on distrust and need, gradually building to an understanding. She could hardly picture him now, several years later. Only impressions remained—scattered words, a hand resting on her face. She didn't need these things from him anymore. But to be understood, that's what she missed the most.

The SU tracks headed east. The opposite direction Jax had led them many years ago. They were returning from somewhere with a destination in mind. Pinot didn't have to think too hard to figure out where that might be. Jax had been betrayed, and if she understood anything about him, it was that he would not let it go lightly. He'd had years for that betrayal to fester inside of him. The destruction left in his wake, it was a portent. A sign of what he would do to those who got in his way.

Pinot scanned the ruins one last time. Her search was at a dead end. No sign of Ed and nobody she could ask. And if Jax's final destination was the restaurant, this might be her only chance to stop him.

Her path lay in the wake of destruction.

Chapter 5
May Paints

It was happening again. The static in her ears, the wash of discordant music tumbling through her head. The middle of the day and she was locked up in her dark bedroom, pretending to sleep off a headache. Lucas wasn't helping. From his crib, he emphasised with her distress, reflecting it back to her in a feedback loop that her ability magnified with each passing minute. Since she'd told Sophie not to affect her son, he'd been starting to pick up on other people's abilities. Hers especially.

Through the crashing sea of emotions, May focused on earlier that morning when Lucas had inexplicably made a copy of his tiny plastic spoon. One minute holding one spoon, the next, one in each hand. Did that mean someone in the restaurant had that power? She tried to picture the people who had been nearby at the time, but the static washed out their features, left them grey outlines.

Gradually, the feedback loop from Lucas faded away as he finally fell asleep. She pushed through the constant hum of the restaurant to find her own body sitting on the side of her too-big mattress. The only queen-sized bed in the restaurant and she was sleeping in it alone.

Her gaze caught on the tin on her bedside table. She turned on the rechargeable lantern and took a square of white paper from the drawer. She'd found it tucked inside one of the encyclopaedias in the gaming room and had been saving it.

She removed the lid of the tin and filled it with water from the wash basin. Moving the nightstand out from the wall, May arranged the pigments, the water, and the paper in front of her. She stared at the paper for a long time.

The half-sized paintbrush was light in her hand, barely there. Did she even remember how to do this?

She'd treat them like watercolours, she decided, and gave the paper a light wash of water. The edges curled. She used Lucas's bottle, a coffee mug, and the two halves of the tin to weigh down the corners. The pigments were grainy and there weren't enough of them. But she managed.

She sat back from the finished painting. The static had eased somewhat and she was able to sort through the emotions a bit easier. Her mind had been working while her attention was absorbed with the kinetic feel of the paintbrush across paper, colours spreading over the page like fire—there was relief, but something more. A remembering. A return. May could feel it, apart from everyone else's emotions crowding in on her.

As she gently blew across the square of paper, May wondered how much longer she could go on like this. She hadn't told anyone about the problems her ability was causing: sleepless nights, static headaches, the potency of Lucas's enhancing power knocking her into emotional spirals. Being alone in her room once Lucas fell asleep was the closest thing she had to a respite. But she wasn't used to being alone. She didn't like it. She missed having coffee with Arissa, gardening with Rhonda and the rest, walking through the woods with Isak…was it worth giving all of that up to prove that she didn't need Sophie's help?

She packed up the paint tin, replaced the nightstand in its spot next to the wall. She placed the mostly dry painting in the drawer and left the shallow tray half-open.

Chapter 6
Pinot and Jax

The SU's trail led east, then veered to the south. Pinot followed them for weeks, picking up supplies in the patches that Jax destroyed on his way. There was a garden in one, a burned husk of a farmhouse in another, a flat expanse with no sign of what had stood there before. As the spring ripened, the snow that Pinot had been using as drinking water melted completely away. She rationed rain, felt herself toughening, adapting as she'd done many times before. At least now there were birds and rabbits to hunt in the greener parts of the wasteland.

After days of following the trail as it sloped to the northeast, Pinot spotted them in the distance. Stipples of bronze ahead of her, growing to mushrooms, then towering mounds. Metal hills. Then, she saw him.

Leaning against the side of one of the SUs, he was familiar. Black hair cut into a short mohawk, the tip cresting over his forehead and breaking into curls. Safety pins lined the edges of his ears. Loose shirt and shorts, bands of metal over each shoulder. His hands-in-pockets posture, the sharp and dangerous grin. His deep brown eyes.

But the years had changed him—his slim figure had filled out into a broader chest, muscular legs. A body that did not know comfort, only survival. And he had survived, she saw—nothing beyond that.

"Well, fuck me," Jax grinned, his sharp eye teeth visible. "It's the Millerite."

"Don't call me that," Pinot growled.

Jax pushed away from the SU with his shoulders. "Makes no difference to me." He studied her. "I'm not going to hurt you."

"No?" Pinot's hands clenched into fists.

Jax shook his head, the safety pins in his ears clicking against each other.

"Just wanna talk?"

"If that's what you want." He took a step towards her, then spread his empty hands. Not a threat.

Pinot didn't take the bait. "I know what you're doing."

"I doubt that," Jax said.

"You're on your way to Arissa's."

He bared his teeth, void of amusement. "And if I am? You should be happy. After everything they did to you. To us!"

"May shouldn't have done what she did."

"And...?" He flipped a hand, waiting for her answer.

"No, Jax."

"And she should be punished." His eyes narrowed. "They all should be!"

"It's different there now. You'd be hurting people you've never even met, people who have nothing to do with this," she appealed to him. "Even May...it's different now!"

"May and Ed manipulated me, Pinot." Jax said softly, his voice lingering on her name. "They messed up my feelings, what I was thinking, making me do things..."

"Not anymore," Pinot said, taking a step towards him. "Not anymore, you're free from all of that, free to go anywhere, do anything."

"But I don't want to be," Jax said. He approached her with an intensity that forced her to back up. "Get it, Millerite? The freedom you're talking about, I don't want it! What's that old saying? *Old sins cast long shadows.* Well, I'm the shadow that's going to go on and on forever, old sins, old sins..."

Pinot's back hit an SU.

And suddenly, he was there, his arms braced on either side of her. Closer than anyone had been since...her back pressed against the cold metal. Jax stood boxing her in, his brown eyes caught in hers.

The old pain spooled through her. "I wish...things could have been different."

After a moment, Jax drew back from her and turned away.

"Jax," Pinot said. "Is it you? Destroying all those places."

Jax opened his arms in a long-suffering gesture. "What do you think?"

"And the Partiers?" The rage filled her as she thought of the starved group clustered outside of the clinic. "You made them live in a nightmare! They were your friends, they were innocent—!"

"Nobody's innocent!" He turned from the wasteland to face her, a crooked grin etched into his face. "You just don't get it! Nothing you say will stop me. Never! So do the smart thing, and stay out of my way!" Sprinting to the side of his SU, Jax caught the rungs on the metal hull and scrambled into the machine. The hatch hissed shut.

"Jax!" she yelled. "You have to stop this! Please!"

The SU horde powered up. The bronze domes whirred into movement and followed Jax's machine as it continued on its way east.

Pinot ran after them until her lungs gave out and her legs cramped. She leaned over, gasping for air, filled with pain.

Log Entry 28:

It was Pinot! I couldn't believe how much older she was, no longer the sharp 17-year-old I remembered from the convenience store. Her hair is cut short now, her clothes worn and grey. I almost disengaged my hatch lock to help her, but Jax let her walk free.

He called me once she left, finally gave me the schematics for the weapon. It's hydrogen-based, frighteningly effective. He demanded that I improve it.

I'm afraid to ask what for. But this is what I needed. With the small hacks I've made into my own S.U. and the schematics, I can work on disarming it without drawing Jax's suspicion. Will it be too late? So many people already killed...

Chapter 7
Ulway in the
Storage Room

Ulway took the full bin from his aunt.

"Thanks," she said, moving to check on a boiling pot on the stove. "I'll make some hot chocolate when you're done."

He carried the bin awkwardly, holding the handle on the left side, cradling it with an angled right arm so the edge of the lid dug into his chest. But he didn't have far to go. He unlocked the storage room door and went inside.

A chair and a long table waited for him in the middle of the room, late afternoon light spilling over the surface from a high window. Stacks of large bins and crates were pyramided against the wall, some supplies set along a built-in workbench at the back of the cramped room.

Ulway set the bin on the chair, wincing as his hitched up shoulder cramped. He took a minute to slowly work out the tension, half-lifting his shoulder in its socket, holding out his arm and making small circles with his wrist. It helped a little bit.

Taking things from the bin, he set them in a neat line on the table. The usual pattern. He and his aunt had come up with the system as a way to make sure nothing was missed.

Once the bin was empty, Ulway returned to the first item in the line: a jar of generator oil. Picking up the jar in his left hand, he felt as the slick liquid sloshed up the inside of the glass and imagined the thick sweet mechanical odour. As soon as he thought of an identical jar in his right hand, it appeared.

He placed both full jars into the bin and moved to the next item. A jar of powdered coffee creamer. The off-white flakes shifted lightly as he picked it up—they'd dissolve in hot liquid, leave it cloudy and sweet. A second, identical jar of creamer filled his hand.

Down the line. A toothbrush. A box of soup base. Kleenexes. A pair of garden gloves.

Sweating, Ulway stopped at the halfway mark. His hands ached. He scanned the remaining items: some soap, a cluster of empty jars, tea bags. These were the things he liked to keep for last. Simple, comforting, fragrant things that would wear him out less.

The light was starting to fade. His aunt had promised him hot chocolate. Wiping his forehead with the sleeve of his oversized jacket, Ulway pressed on.

A knock on the storage room door interrupted him. Thinking it had to be his aunt—no one else knew he was in there—he unlocked it and returned to the table.

"Are you duplicating things?" Ksenia's voice came from behind him. "I knew that's what you were doing!"

Ulway whipped around, almost knocking the glass jars onto the floor. "You're," he cleared his throat, "you're not supposed to be here. Nobody's supposed to know."

"Where do they think all this stuff comes from?" Ksenia tapped the top of one of the jars.

"Traders?" Ulway said, at a loss. He'd never thought of that.

Ksenia came around the table to look in the almost-full bin. Since they'd been caught planning to leave the restaurant, it had been weird. His aunt had told him to be careful around her. He didn't know what that meant. But with Ksenia moving the bin to sit in his chair, wearing her soft blue shirt and handmade brown skirt and boots, her wrists festooned with bright friendship bracelets, he discovered he didn't want to be careful.

With Ksenia watching, he duplicated the jars all the way to the box of tea bags at the end of the line.

"This place is named after you, isn't it?" she asked.

"Oh. Not really." Ulway's cheeks warmed. "It was my parents last name. Mine too."

"Ulway's not your first name?"

"No."

"What is it?"

"Theodore. But I don't like it." Ulway felt lightheaded. He awkwardly sat on one of the stacks of bins against the wall. These big "restocking" days always wore him out.

Ksenia crossed her ankles out in front of her, frowning. "It's unfair that you have to hide all this. You're the one keeping this place running. And it's named after you. It's your place, you should get to make the rules."

Ulway started to protest, having to stop in order to clear his throat again. He needed a drink. He was tired. His shoulder ached. It was unfair.

Ksenia shuffled the chair closer, tapping her bracelets against his wrist. "You're not mad at me, are you? I'm sorry we got caught."

Ulway tried to sit up a little straighter. "I could never be mad at you."

"That's sweet," Ksenia smiled, showing her square front teeth. "It's so dumb that I have to help teach that ASL class."

Ulway laughed. "You're great," he said, then mumbled, "at it, at teaching stuff."

Ksenia placed a hand on his. "Want to learn?"

The pressure and warmth of her hand surprised him. "Um," he said, nervously noticing the window. "It's late, my aunt might come in to see how I'm doing."

She was so close to him. Ulway closed his eyes, overcome by a moment of fatigue and warm satisfaction. When he opened his eyes, Ksenia's face was inches away. He could make out each of her freckles. Before he could blink, she kissed his cheek.

Ksenia started up, her hand leaving his. "We'll keep it a secret," she said, taking a handful of tea bags from the bin. "Can I have these?"

Ulway nodded, then watched her open the door, scan the hall, and leave.

Once the warmth of her lips on his cheek completely faded, Ulway gathered up the bin and left the storage room, locking it behind him.

"Oh, Ulway," Arissa said as she spotted him across the dining hall. "I was just about to see if you needed some help." She took the bin from him, leading the way into the kitchen.

Ulway followed, bracing himself against the counter. "Aunty," he said as she scooped hot chocolate powder—powder that he'd duplicated hundreds of times in the seven years since the Event—into two mugs of hot water. "Why can't I tell people?"

"About what?" she said, stirring the hot chocolate with a spoon that he'd made.

"That I keep this place running?" he echoed Ksenia's words.

Arissa glanced over at him, her dark brown eyes narrowing. "You can't tell people because it's dangerous. Remember? There are people out there on the wasteland," she closed her eyes for a moment, "if they knew what you could do, they might try and take you away."

Ulway shuddered at the nightmares his aunt's reasoning gave him. "But even the people here, even our friends don't know. I don't," he coughed to clear his throat. "I don't think that's fair."

"Maybe not, but it's the rules, okay?" She placed the hot chocolate in front of him. "And you can't tell Ksenia." Her voice grew hard. "I know she's nice to you, but you have to be careful."

Ulway stared into the mug. "I'll be careful."

"Love you," his aunt said.

Ulway carried his hot chocolate into the dining hall. There was a candle on the table he sat at, a candle he'd made dozens of copies of. He sipped at his drink, the warm sweetness coating his mouth, making him drowsy. Candlelight flickered over his friendship bracelet, changing it from yellow to orange to red.

Chapter 8
Arissa and the Fire

The intention was travelling over distances, a clanging bell that reverberated through Arissa, down to her bones.

"Something's coming." Arissa stood up from where Rhonda was helping her weed the garden.

"Something bad?" Rhonda asked, brushing the dirt from her gloves.

Arissa gripped Rhonda's arm. "Rhonda," she said, keeping her voice calm. "I want you to go in through the back entrance. Tell everyone that they have to hide in the woods, right now. Don't let anyone go out the front. Clear?"

Frightened by Arissa's warning, Rhonda freed her arm. "Yes, I'll go right now."

"Run!" Arissa yelled after Rhonda. "Run!"

The ringing grew closer, almost arrived—familiar. Arissa moved towards the enmity as if through a fog, setting steady steps on the path to the front of the restaurant. She reached the middle of the gravel drive, sensing the open hatred of the approaching threat. There was no need to listen beyond the one pulsing intention—it rang out, deep and clear and dangerous.

The first SU crested the gravel road with the rest in tow, a bronze-clad army on her doorstep. One of the machines drew next to her and stopped.

Arissa held her ground as the hatch opened and Jax climbed

down to meet her.

"Still kicking?" He bared his sharpened eye teeth.

"Jax," Arissa acknowledged him, probing with her ability. His intention spiked down through every layer of his being. "Pinot isn't here."

"I know," he said, arrogant in his knowledge, his power.

"What do you want?" Arissa asked, hoping a delay would be enough for everyone to get out of the restaurant.

"You let them stay here, knowing what they were. Murderers, manipulators." Jax grinned. "You deserve this as much as any of them."

Arissa shuddered at the malice in his words.

"Remember that."

He was waiting for something, Arissa realised. "No—!"

A rip in the sky, a boom that exploded through her head, blocking vision, blocking action. Her knees hit gravel, hands over her ears.

Jax stood silhouetted next to her, laughing, hands overhead, tears streaming down his face.

The restaurant. The restaurant was burning.

Arissa pushed herself off the ground, everything in her drawing her towards her home, her family. Now there was no fear, nothing, only action. The flames roared ahead, licking at the wooden beams holding up the sign, heavy smoke spilling out of the restaurant's door. She zipped her coat up over her nose and jumped into the inferno, looking for anyone in the blaze, anyone at all. The smoke filled her eyes, and she dropped down to crawl along the curling linoleum. She couldn't see anyone.

"Ulway!" she yelled, her voice lost in the roar and the heat and the haze. "Ulway!"

The smoke overwhelmed her. She backed up, coughing, scrambling to her feet.

She ran out of the entryway and around the side of the building to the back door. She wrenched it open, white smoke pouring out of it.

"No, no, no." She tried to go in, but the smoke caught in her throat, she couldn't breathe. She stumbled back, hands twisting her jacket, tears and ash and sweat coating her face.

There was nothing she could do. Only offer herself to what remained.

Arissa drew herself up and watched as *Ulway's Restaurant and Retreat Centre* burned and burned and burned.

Chapter 9
Rhonda and the Fire

Rhonda ran to the back door as Arissa's instructions rang in her ears. She burst into the large communal sleeping area she shared with half a dozen other residents.

Sophie was sitting on her bed, reading. "What's wrong?" she asked.

"Everyone has to run through the back door." Rhonda gulped air. "Into the forest, no one out the front."

Taking charge, Sophie sprung up from the bed and headed into the hallway. "I'll take the upstairs, you take the other rooms down here. And make sure May knows!"

Rhonda kicked her bag free from underneath her cot, scooping it up as she ran to May's room. She wrenched the door open. "May! We have to go! Take Lucas into the woods!"

"What?" May sat up from the queen-sized bed. Her tired and pale face suddenly filled with horror. "Oh no." Stumbling over to the crib, May scooped up Lucas and pushed past Rhonda, booking it for the back door.

"Everybody!" Rhonda called into the sleeping areas as she hurried down the hall. "Emergency! Out the back way, into the woods, as fast as you can!"

The residents went into action, stuffing belongings into bags, panic filling the air.

"Ulway! Ksenia!" Rhonda yelled across to the open games

room. "Out back, now!"

After checking the bathroom and the storage area, Rhonda rushed to the back door, out of breath, anxiously waiting for people to join her. Sophie wasn't back, and she hadn't seen anyone else come down the stairs.

Scattered footsteps echoed overhead. Then, a muffled boom, like a far off thunderclap. The air was sucked out from around her. No sound. Rhonda jumped out of the back door and started running, just as a stream of fire roared over the entire restaurant.

The heat was intense. She was metres away, and she could still feel it roasting her alive, sizzling the air around her. The trees above her groaned and crackled. The forest she'd spent two years getting to know was burning.

A log in the underbrush tripped her up and sent her sprawling. Her bag pulled awkwardly at her arm as it slid up around her hair. She took deep breaths, waiting for feeling to come back into her legs.

The smell of dead leaves and damp moss reached her through the smoke. The creek. If the forest was burning, she'd follow the water.

Pushing herself up, she stumbled down the slope towards the creek. Before she could reach it, she saw them.

The massive bronze domes filed down the road from the restaurant in a solemn procession, their hundreds of eyes glowing white. She'd only read about them in Ed's notes, heard the stories, but she knew what they were. Survival Units.

She crouched behind a cluster of young trees, watching the SUs as they continued down the road leading to the southern wasteland. The ground underneath her hummed as they passed.

When the SUs were gone, Rhonda crossed the road and found the place in the creek where the river ran low, leaving rocks for a crossing. She waited on the bank, looking up at where the restaurant burned, the trees going up in an inferno that no one could quench.

She waited for people, waited for them to come out from

the trees and tell her this was all some kind of game, that the restaurant wasn't really on fire. She waited alone on the bank until night came.

A fine rain misted over the forest, building into sheets of water that pummelled her back and took her breath away. The fire hissed and sent huge clouds of smoke to combat the rain, but the water shredded through the clouds as if they were nothing at all.

The storm passed. The night filled with silent starlight reflecting off the creek that murmured secrets at her side. Rhonda was soaked, and the cold shivered through her as she hugged her backpack to her chest, everything that was left to her.

Why was this happening? And in the next breath, *It didn't matter.*

Rhonda heard footsteps approaching. Arissa came through the trees and stopped at the edge of the creek bank. Her black and grey hair was curling as it dried, but her clothes were soaked from the rain and covered in charred smudges.

"Where is everyone?" Rhonda asked. "Why aren't they here?"

Arissa gave Rhonda a hand up, pulling her into a tight hug. "Come on," Arissa said as Rhonda held onto her shoulder. "We'll go to the cabin."

Log Entry 33:

The restaurant.

Jax made sure I didn't know where we were until it was too late. He got out to meet the woman standing in the road. I couldn't hear them.

Then the boom of the weapon, the red bloom of fire on my screens.

Jax was still outside, enjoying his handiwork. The woman's orange flare rushed towards the storm of red, joining it.

I managed to erase the survivor's readings trailing from the back of the restaurant into the woods. Jax will see them wink out on the replay, as if they died trying to escape. I only hope that's enough.

Chapter 10
Ulway and the Fire

Flames blazed behind him, a groaning, cracking, splitting roar that he could feel from his feet to the top of his head. And heat, melting, liquifying, unwavering heat rolling over him in waves. The trees cast matchstick shadows over each other, swaggering back and forth like a drunken army.

"We have to keep going!" Ksenia said when Ulway stopped, petrified by the intensity of the fire behind them and the shadowy trees ahead.

They made it to the end of the acre behind the restaurant where the land dropped off and a small ridge protruded from the steep incline. Ksenia led Ulway down to it, then took a length of rope from her backpack. She stabbed a tent peg into the earth and pulled on the knot already tied through the peg's metal eye. It held. "Okay, nice and slow." She positioned Ulway facing the steep incline, placing his hands around the rope. "Go down backwards," she said. "I'll hold it." She picked up the slack between them.

Without thinking, Ulway did as she said, setting one foot behind him and clinging onto the rope, before moving another step backwards. The incline wasn't steep enough to make him climb down, but it was close. He breathed in relief when he found himself among trees on level ground. Shading his eyes from the red light spilling over the ridge, he spotted Ksenia. She backed down the steep wall, a slim shadow against the grey shale.

With a scraping sound and a ringing of metal hitting stone, the tent peg came loose and flew off the ridge, taking the rope with it. Ksenia rolled the last couple metres down the incline until a tree stopped her.

Ulway's heart fell into his stomach as he rushed over to her. She was curled on the forest floor, laughing.

"Oh my god, I was so scared!" she gasped, then laughed again.

Ulway laughed uncertainly as she brushed herself off and stuffed the rope back into her bag. He stepped towards her to pick a branch out of her hair.

Ksenia smiled up at him, then used the tree to stand. "Let's go!" She headed off into the forest, Ulway following after her.

"Where?" Ulway said, the trees around him unfamiliar. The roar of the fire was a dim rustle somewhere behind them and the red light had thinned to the grey twilight of his bedroom window. It made the world surreal, not quite there. Maybe he was dreaming.

"Ulway," Ksenia stopped and took his hand. "I know that your aunt was convincing, but she was lying, okay? The colony is nothing like that. My mom made all that stuff up."

Ulway remembered Catherine's scars. "No she didn't."

"There's a cow, remember? And parties? And my friends."

"I'm your friend," Ulway said.

"Of course you are," she said. "That's why I want you to come with me. Please?"

"But what if they make you marry that cruel man, and they make me do things?"

"They won't! They won't because it was all a lie!" She paused and frowned. "Even if it's not a lie, Mom deserved it. The first time she tried to run away, everyone told me she was a bad woman, a very bad woman. I swore I would never be bad. I was happy there until Mom took me away. I want to go back. I'm not bad. And if I bring you with me, they'll see that. They'll throw us both a party!"

Ulway stood surrounded by trees as Ksenia laughed. Her short sandy-brown hair, her freckles, her square teeth, all of them were dear to him. He thought about never seeing her again, and his insides felt empty. "You were planning to run away," he realised. "That's why you had the rope in your bag."

"I have enough food for both of us, and you can duplicate more, right?" She touched her wrist to his. "It'll only take a week or so to get there."

"I can't go with you," he said. "I promised."

"You promised me," she said forcefully. "You said you'd come."

"No," Ulway decided. "I'm going to find my aunt."

"She's probably dead!" Ksenia spat. "They're probably all dead, and you'll find out, and be all alone. You'll wish you came along with me!"

Ulway hesitated, his eyes filling with tears.

"You know what? You're boring. You're all boring!" Ksenia stomped her way through the trees until Ulway couldn't hear her anymore.

Left alone in the woods, Ulway wiped the tears out of his eyes. The night was heavy around him, with unfamiliar smells and sounds. He turned around with a small whimper. The dull red glow remained over the black trees, the hunk of ridge the size of a block he could lift with one hand. He had to find his aunt.

Ulway coughed to clear his throat. He was very thirsty. He picked his way slowly through the woods, using the red firelight as a guide. A rustle in the underbrush stopped him in his tracks, the moving leaves propelling his heart into a stampede rhythm. His high shoulder cramped, but he didn't dare stretch it out.

Waiting for something to come out of the trees, Ulway took a shallow breath through his nose. "Ksenia? Are you there?" He slowly backed away from where the noise had come from and gave it a wide berth as he realigned his path.

Smoke filled the air, obscuring the stars overhead. He reached the ridge, the scree-covered slope rising up like a wall.

He paused to massage his tensed shoulder and rub his sore and watery eyes.

More familiar with the area, Ulway turned to the left, where there was a path running along the creek. He made his way slowly through the darkness, sometimes slipping on the damp creek bank. His stomach rumbled, tears ran freely from his red eyes trying to clear the smoke and ash. *The restaurant is gone*, he told himself but kept going anyway.

He angled up the gravel path to the front of the restaurant. The log-sided building that his parents had built in the middle of the woods—their pride and joy, his home since the Event—was a burning skeleton of charred wood and matchstick-thin boards consumed by flames.

Ulway turned away and only got a few steps before he threw up on the gravel between his feet. Ksenia was right. He was all alone.

He crouched on the ground, shuffling away from the puddle of vomit. He cried into his knees.

When it began to rain, he blinked up into it and took a deep shuddering breath.

He had to find a safe place. The closest one was the cabin where May and Isak used to live. His aunt had told him if anything happened to the restaurant, to her, he should go to the cabin.

He couldn't move.

The rain eventually stopped, and still he sat there, curled in a ball, not looking at the ruins.

Finally, he pushed himself up from the gravel and closed his eyes until he was facing away from the restaurant. When he opened them, they felt clear. He could see the creek gleaming in the starlight. He walked to it, found the little crossing and made it to the other side. He saw the path that led to the cabin.

Ulway froze at the path's opening. What if there were Grafters there, bad people, like the one who'd almost killed May last fall? Worse: what if there was nobody else there? Everyone dead—his parents, his aunt, his friends. What if Ksenia was right?

Then he saw the candle in the window. The same as the restaurant. A welcome.

He stumbled towards the cabin and caught the railing to help him up onto the porch. He thumped his thick hand against the dry wood of the front door. "Aunty!" he cried.

The door opened. "Theodore!" Arissa said. "My Ulway, come in, you're here, thank God."

He sat on the couch as his aunt wiped the rain from his face and wrapped a blanket over his uneven shoulders.

"Are you okay?" he managed to ask her.

"Yes, my dear," she said. "I'm so glad you're alright."

"Aunty," Ulway said. "I want to stay with you."

"I know, Ulway." She sat next to him. "I can see that you have something else you want to tell me."

Ulway reached a hand to his shoulder then dropped it. "I... I want it to be different this time. I want people to know what I can do."

"Oh, my dear," his aunt said, pulling him into a hug.

Ulway hugged her back. "I don't want to hide, Aunty."

"You're absolutely right," she said. "From now on, no more hiding."

Chapter 11
Pinot and the Saint

Pinot lost track of time as she followed the SUs' trail. Walk, eat, sleep for a couple hours, repeat. Only one goal: to stop Jax, to get to Arissa's before him, by some miracle, some bending of space-time. Why couldn't the Event have given her that power instead? Instant travel. So much better than her slow and gross healing ability. She was carrying her spit around in plastic sandwich bags, for fucksakes. Clem had provided them as a more palatable option for people on the wasteland who didn't want someone literally spitting on them. But she hadn't had the opportunity to put their hypothesis to the test. She hadn't seen another human being since her run in with Jax.

Pinot found herself in an area of wasteland that was dead—no vegetation or soil to keep track of the SUs' passing. A rainstorm exploded over the bare land, blowing her off-course and leaving her drenched. She kept walking in a direction that felt like east, sheets of water forcing her to keep her eyes closed. When the rain cleared, she pulled the compass from inside her soaked jacket and found that she'd spent the past few hours heading north.

"Fuck." Pinot ruffled her short hair, shaking the water free. No use trying to camp in the water-logged barren land. She re-oriented herself, heading south-east in hopes that she'd soon be able to see Arissa's forest in the distance.

The sun touched the horizon behind her. Her shadow stretched long ahead, a shade over the red-gold earth. There was moss underfoot, she realised. Ahead were lush ferns and even bushes rising from the ground. Beyond them, in the twilight, a low building of some kind. Getting closer, Pinot proceeded cautiously, listening for any movement around the stone courtyard with a long structure along the far wall.

No one stopped her. She reached the courtyard, cobblestones uneven underfoot. Ivy curled up over the grey stone arches to the curved red shingles.

Hearing something move in one of the shadowed arches, Pinot froze, trying to locate the source. Rustling around the ivy. Suddenly, the creature emerged—small, black, furry.

Pinot relaxed. It was just a stray cat. Mangy thing, scruffy, but with clean paws. It meowed at Pinot. She stayed on her guard. The cat wove between her hiking boots, tail up along her leg in greeting. It sat and curled its tail around its feet and looked up at her with round gold and black eyes.

"Alright, alright," Pinot crouched down. She extended a hand to the cat, who enthusiastically responded, leaning into Pinot's palm so far that it teetered off-balance.

Pinot laughed as it righted itself and pushed at her hand again. "You don't seem to be sick or anything." She smoothed the rough fur on the cat's triangular head. "And I guess I'm immune to most things, so what've I got to lose?" She settled down in the scrub grass and scratched behind its ears. When she tried to work through a tangled tuft on its back, the cat arched against the pressure with a low growl. "Don't like that, okay, noted." Pinot returned to stroking the cat's ears and it relaxed, settling against Pinot's knee.

"Found a friend?" a voice whispered directly in her ear.

Pinot jumped to her feet, the cat running off with a yowl. Pinot scanned the courtyard, but it was empty.

"You didn't forget about me already, did you?" the silver voice teased.

Pinot felt a thrill run up her spine, a rush of air in her chest.

She raised her arms ahead of her like a zombie, heading to where the voice had come from.

"Over here!" the voice called.

Pinot swung her arms and shambled towards the shadowed arch leading into the hall. Not finding anything, she dropped the zombie bit and continued down the corridor. A candle burned at the far end of the hall, casting shadows onto moth-eaten tapestries and old oak furniture. "Welcome to the saint's abode!"

Pinot smirked. "A saint, huh?"

"Get on thy knees, pilgrim," announced a magnanimous voice. "Receive the blessing of Irene, the Saint of the Wastes."

"For a fee?" Pinot knelt on the stone floor.

"You may leave an offering," Irene's husky voice replied. "After you receive my blessing."

Pinot closed her eyes in mock reverence.

Irene's warm lips pressed against her forehead.

"You have been blessed!" Irene sang, the room reverberating with the sound. "My priest! Where is my priest?"

A hooded figure appeared from an alcove next to the altar.

"Ah, come hither my priest—"

"'Come hither!'" Pinot snorted.

"—and receive the offering!" Irene finished as scathingly as possible.

Pinot played the part of the penitent worshipper, taking a scavenged hammer from her bag and handing it over to the 'priest'.

"Go now, in peace, good pilgrim." Irene said, her voice fading away. "You will have...good fortune..."

After a moment, the three of them broke into laughter.

"This is fucking gold," Pinot laughed, falling back onto her butt, tears streaming down her face.

"And it works more often than you would think," the 'priest' said in a deep resonant voice, letting the hood of the robe fall back. They were in their 40s and had a modest beard speckled with grey.

"This is Tanner, by the way," Irene's voice returned to her

usual silvery light tone. "He's my partner in this escapade. Tanner, this is Pinot."

"A pleasure to meet you," Tanner said with a small bow.

"So, 'Saint of the Wastes'." Pinot shook her head. "Makes sense why you left *Between Breads*. It's a good gig."

"Oh, you didn't see it, did you?" Irene said, her voice moving closer to Tanner. "It was destroyed."

Pinot felt her mouth go dry. "Burned?"

"Yes," Irene said. "A few months ago. Streams of fire, bronze domes in the distance. Your friend Jax making a move, I think."

"I'm tracking him."

"Well, you can't track him through the night," Irene said. "Stay with us. You need a change of clothes. We don't have a lot of food, but it's warm enough."

"Alright," Pinot said, comfortably submitting to Irene's directive. The thrill was back in her spine. She wondered what Irene looked like after their year apart.

The three of them went back down the corridor, passing the courtyard. The cat was nowhere to be seen.

Tanner unlocked a small wooden door with a skeleton key. The cloth robe he wore stirred around his torso, an invisible arm wrapping around it.

"We were very lucky to find this place," Irene said. "We think it was an old church, or even a historical re-creation of a monastery. Everything's made to look old, and there's no light fixtures or switches or outlets. Just places for candles to go."

"I went to one of those heritage parks when I was a kid," Pinot said. "There'd be actors dressed up, making horseshoes and stuff."

"Yeah, exactly like that!" Tanner replied with generous enthusiasm. "There's a costume room through the other hall. We found some tools in the lockers, instruction binders for the actors. We've made the most of it."

Pinot felt a pull forward on her arm as Irene drew her through the wooden door. Tanner moved around the room lighting candles with a taper. Dusty furniture and sparsely decorated walls appeared out of the darkness. A four-poster bed rose from the centre of the room.

"Over here," Irene said as a chair moved from under a stocky dining table. "I'll see what I have…"

Pinot sat in the chair as Irene's voice mumbled from a wardrobe on the other side of the room. A stack of clothes hovered over to the four poster bed. "Oof!" Irene exclaimed as she tossed them onto the duvet. "It's seriously a fashion show over here," she said. "I found a couple things in your size— honestly, your clothes are worn to shit. I know you're travelling across the wasteland, but that doesn't mean you have to look like a ghoul."

"A ghoul!" Pinot laughed, matching eyes with Tanner across the room. His eyebrows raised in shared amusement.

"Ahem," Irene brought the focus back to the pile of clothes. "Jeans, a little old, but in better shape than what you're wearing right now. A t-shirt, sweater, spare socks, etc. And this." The clothes pile collapsed as Irene pulled something free. "I thought this was more your style." A leather jacket with a flipped collar, brass zippers, and deep pockets rose to around where Irene's torso would be. "Waterproof and lined for cooler weather."

"Perfect," Pinot smiled.

"Perfect," Irene agreed. Her footsteps echoed on the stone floor as the jacket drifted over to the table. Irene's invisible hand curled around Pinot's wet jacket sleeve, drawing her over to the pile of clothes. "You should change. There's a curtained area just over there."

"Right." Pinot gathered the pile of items and took them to the corner of the room blocked off with a faded tapestry. As she shed her wet clothes, she studied the woven images of flattened horses and a row of identical faces angled up at a beaming figure.

The jeans were a little big, but everything else was a good fit. "What do you think?" Pinot asked as she returned to the main room.

"Much better!" Irene cheered from a chair at the end of the table.

Pinot hung her wet clothes over a brass bar by the door. She returned to her seat at the table and draped the leather jacket behind her.

"Bon appétit!" Tanner said, setting a wooden plate and goblet in front of Pinot. The plate was covered in greens, cherry tomatoes, and a bread roll. Pinot's mouth literally watered. She lifted the bread roll and smelled it. Water, yeast, sugar, flour, oil, salt. Heat. Bread. Was she dreaming? She took a bite, chewed it slowly. Nothing would ever taste as good. Until the next bite. And the next.

Tanner moved to pick up another set of cups and plates from a sideboard and returned to the table, his robe billowing around his legs.

"You've outdone yourself!" Irene said as he placed a full plate in front of her. A wooden fork hovered above the plate and speared a cherry tomato.

"We don't get many guests," Tanner said as he sat across from Pinot, his own plate and goblet already in place. "At least, not the good kind."

"Thank you." Pinot swallowed the last bit of bread. She took a sip from the goblet and coughed.

"It's beer!" Tanner smiled. "This place has a brewery set-up in the cellar. I guess the monks liked their homebrew."

Pinot took another sip, enjoying the bright yeasty flavour now that she knew what it was. "The monks had a garden too?" Pinot asked, digging into the assortment of vegetables and herbs on her plate.

"Sure did!" Tanner took a long draught from his goblet.

"A little garden of Eden!" Irene said with a laugh. A forkful of greens disappeared into her mouth.

The meal was over sooner than Pinot would've liked. She drained the last of her beer with something like sorrow. Jax weighed on her mind. What if she was too late to stop him?

She started as an invisible hand lowered onto her shoulder.

"Thank you, Tanner," Irene said.

"Was nice to have company." Tanner nodded to Pinot. He started to clear the table, stacking the dishes in a wicker bin. "It's okay," he smiled when Pinot started to help. "You can relax."

"Come visit!" Irene called. The duvet on the four-poster bed was crumpled under her invisible weight.

Pinot approached the bed. "Can I see you?"

"You know how this works," Irene said.

Pinot leaned forward, resting her hands on the silk duvet. She waited for the familiar pressure across her collarbone and Irene's mouth to fix onto her neck. A brief pull of blood, barely enough for Pinot to register. The pressure eased and Pinot took a step back.

Irene was only partly there. Long dark hair loose over her shoulders, green eyes, a gap between her two front teeth. Pinot could make out the rich gold and red duvet through her body, a transparent impression of her, barely an outline.

"I have to stay invisible for the saint thing to work," Irene said with the ghost of a smile. "I only drew enough for tonight."

Pinot looked over as the robed figure left the room. "Does Tanner—?"

"It's good to see you," Irene interrupted, taking her hand. "I always wondered what happened to you and your friend."

Pinot stretched out next to Irene. "Long story."

"I want to hear it." Irene traced a hand over Pinot's forehead. "But you need to sleep. How long have you been out there?"

Pinot tipped her head towards the door. "Won't Tanner be back?"

"He's actually into all of this 'priest of the wasteland saint' stuff. Sleeps in one of the cells like a regular old monk." Irene turned onto her side, candles flickering through her long dark hair. "We have some catching up to do."

"Yes." Pinot kissed her. "Yes. Yes."

"You can stay," Irene said. "You could be another priest, do minor healing miracles for me."

"That's okay." Pinot said in her ear. "You're doing just fine here, I think."

"You're right," Irene smiled tenderly. "People might start venerating you instead of me."

"Saints aren't supposed to be jealous."

"I'm glad...that I got to see you...again..."

"Mmm."

"Leaving in the morning?"

"Soon as it's light enough to see...I'll get out of your hair."

"Tomorrow," Irene whispered. "Tomorrow."

Chapter 12
Isak After the Fire

Isak recognized her. The figure standing ahead of him, burned remnants of the restaurant framing her, the wasteland beyond dyed red with dying sunlight.

"Isn't this what you wanted?" Pinot turned to ask him. "For everything to be over? That's why you jumped, right? The fire must've been intense. I—" Pinot frowned, her hands clenching in the deep pockets of her leather jacket. "I didn't get here in time."

The memory of the fire washed over Isak and he gripped his knees to keep himself from keeling over. "Oh God," he moaned, half-bent over in the burned remnants of his former home. "What happened? Did everyone... did Lucas...?"

Pinot shook her head. "I don't know."

Isak's sobs overwhelmed any further questions he wanted to ask. He held his stomach and tried to stop his body from shaking. After a while, his vision cleared and his voice was his own again.

"How long ago?" he asked.

"A few days, at least."

Isak stiffly sat on a burned tree trunk. He hadn't jumped more than a day in years, and now his survival instincts had come to the rescue, bringing him out of harm's way, leaving everyone else behind. He remembered the smoke-saturated air burning in his lungs, the intense flames roaring up on all sides. He'd been alone. Maybe May and Lucas and the others had already escaped. But in retrospect, he had to accept the truth—in the moment, he'd only cared about himself.

"Oh God," he whispered, repeating it over and over as a way to keep from falling completely to pieces.

Pinot watched him for a while, then sighed. Squatting next to him, she checked his injuries. "Here," she placed something into his hand, "you'll need this to prevent infection." Then she went further into the ruins to sift through the debris.

After the sky had gone from red to grey to black, Isak came to himself again. He opened his hand and found a sealed plastic bag labelled *Anti-septic*. "You keep your spit in bags now?" he asked the darkness.

"People in Summerland seemed to like it better," Pinot said from behind him.

Isak applied some of the salve to his arms. *That's right*, he remembered. With Pinot outside of Sophie's dampening influence, her powers would return in full force.

He dropped the plastic bag. *Sophie*. If he'd jumped days into the future, that meant…

Sophie was gone. Who else would he have to mourn in the coming days? What if Lucas…what if May…?

With a huge effort, Isak managed to turn around and shuffle over to the makeshift lean-to Pinot had constructed with some old beams and a tarp. The ground held warmth from the burned-down building; occasionally, he heard a crack of wood still smouldering underneath the charred remains around them.

Without speaking, they each laid down on their side of the shelter.

"Remember the crutches?" Pinot said after a while.

He pictured a 17-year-old Pinot swinging herself between two adult-sized crutches. "All those foot races around the convenience store."

"You let me win."

"Well, you let me win at chess, so we're even."

"I guess we are," Pinot said with extra weight, as if something else had occurred to her.

Isak understood her meaning. "We helped with your burns. Now, you're helping me with mine."

"It's funny, that's all," Pinot said seriously. "Almost enough to make you believe in karma."

"Why'd you come back?" Isak asked.

Pinot shifted on the ground. "I found out Jax was heading this way...I hoped that Arissa would've been able to talk him down...But, she's not here, is she?" Pinot sat up, the shadow of her back and hair barely visible in the dark. "I found some bodies."

Isak stared up at the tarp over them, preparing for the worst. "Whose?"

"Couldn't tell. Too burned. Adults, though." When Isak didn't reply, Pinot lay back down, keeping her distance.

Isak dug under his shirt, wincing as the cloth rubbed his burned arm. He pulled out his icon, held it to his lips, and prayed.

Chapter 13
Pinot in the Ruins

She swore she'd never go back to the restaurant, and yet there she was—in the ruins. Isak was asleep under the tarp she'd set up the night before, snoring. She'd always had a soft spot for Isak. When they first met, out of everyone at the convenience store, she'd felt the most safe with him. Playing chess. Running foot races around the gas pumps. In an odd way, they were good times. It was before Jax had broken into her life.

Pinot sighed. This was exactly why she didn't want to come back. Too many memories churned up from the swamp of the past. She was the one churning them up, she knew, knee-deep in sludge prodding under the murky water with a pole, pulling up weeds and old clothes. They brought her no joy. But it was inevitable, the remembering. Having to face what she'd left behind here. Too many things.

Standing where the restaurant's front door would be, Pinot studied the road leading down and away through the forest. It would be easier for Jax to take the SUs down the road instead of trying to thread them through the trees. Sure enough, there were thick trails in the ash, moving down to join the gravel road that led to the highway. Where was Jax going next?

Where from? she wondered. During their brief encounter, he hadn't mentioned anything about the west coast—nothing about the ocean.

She suddenly smelt his salty breath, felt his arms on either side of her. Years apart, and mere moments of his presence did this to her? Nostalgia was a bitch.

But Jax was responsible for the wreckage behind her. And the bodies she had found were casualties of his rage. She hated him for it and hated herself for not stopping it. For not seeking him out earlier. Because she knew that her old self, in charge of twenty-odd machines and with an unpunished enemy, would have done the same thing.

So where did that leave her? Jax on a killing spree, Isak injured, and most of the restaurant residents MIA. She should leave, while she still had the strength to walk away.

Isak moaned in his sleep, then sat up slowly. "Pinot?"

She settled down next to him. "You're still in bad shape." She took a bread roll out of her pack and handed it to him. "Eat. Rest."

Isak received the roll with amazement. "Where did you get bread?"

Pinot shrugged.

Isak chewed through a couple of bites. "You're not going to tell me where you've been all this time?"

Pinot raised her eyebrows.

"Humour an injured old man."

"You're not that old," Pinot crossed her arms. "What are you, like 40?"

"Thereabouts." Isak popped the last bit of bread into his mouth.

"I guess that's kind of old. Lucky you, to have survived so long."

"Soon I'll go completely grey," Isak said, shaking his shoulder-length black hair from his eyes. His attempt at a smile was pained.

"Well," Pinot thought back. "I left here in the fall. Travelled around a bit. Wintered out past Summerland in a garage, then in the spring…" She swallowed, passed a hand over her short hair. "Something happened to Ed. I came back around here looking for him. He...didn't make it back, did he?"

"Not that I know of. We all thought you'd headed west and spent the winter in Summerland."

Reaching into her backpack, Pinot pulled out another bag of 'antiseptic'. "Late spring, I was at the cabin a few weeks, then got run out of there—"

"That was you?" Isak said.

"Yeah. Didn't want Arissa knowing I stayed around, so I left pretty quick. Arms, please."

Isak shifted to sit facing her and held out his burned arms.

Pinot used two fingers to scoop her spit out of the bag and spread it over the more serious blisters. "I spent the early summer in the woods. It was a good time. Not always easy. But got me back on my feet. A couple Foragers came through—"

"Foragers?"

"Like Grafters, only, I dunno, with a permanent camp and shared leadership? They told me I might get news of Ed in Summerland. Wintered there...then...found out Jax was around and figured he'd be heading this way. That brings us to now, I guess." Pinot wiped her hand on her jeans and tucked the empty spit bag in her backpack.

"You were on the move a lot." Isak lowered his arms, wincing. "It must have been difficult, on your own."

"Sometimes."

"And Ed?"

"Dunno." Pinot cleared her throat. "If he didn't come back here, then I'm out of ideas. Either he's been taken somewhere else or he's..." Pinot didn't finish the sentence. She stood up, taking on her old doctor's manner. "We should drink something."

Pinot took her empty canteen and walked down the gravel drive, through the trees to the creek's edge. It was running, clear and pure as she remembered from her summer in the woods. She greeted it in her mind as she took up the water in her hands.

Pinot filled the canteen and spit in it before screwing on the lid. She splashed water over her face and tried to wash the ashes from under her nails.

What should she do next? All her leads on Ed ended at the decimated prison facility. Did he escape? In that case, it would make more sense to wait for him here. But Jax was out there, dangerous. Would he return west? And Isak. Where would he go? Did any of these people even concern her?

Of course they did. She knew that now. As much as she tried to stay away, she was drawn back in. *Old sins cast long shadows*, Jax had said. But he was wrong. It was the past itself casting the shadows on the ground ahead of her. There was no moving on from this, no real future for her, until she faced them.

She decided to start with the switchblade. She'd carried it with her since finding it at the facility, the twisted, fused weapon. At first, she'd kept it in her pocket, but her hand would forget, go to the pocket for warmth, and find the cold hunk of metal against her knuckles. Keeping it in the bottom of her bag wasn't much better. It rested heavily against her back, in her mind.

She hadn't found Ed in time. She hadn't saved him.

The truth echoed through her as she walked back up the hill.

She sat next to Isak and handed him the full canteen. He gulped down a couple of mouthfuls and gave it back to her.

"The cabin," Isak said suddenly.

Pinot understood. "We'll head over once you've had a chance to rest."

Isak hesitated. "Do you think they'll be there?"

Pinot took a last draught and capped the canteen. "We'll have to see."

Isak raised a hand to his chest, then hid his face.

Pinot took the switchblade out of her bag. "Try to rest. I'll be right back."

She headed into the trees, circling around to the other edge of the burn, where Isak wouldn't be able to see her.

Using the twisted switchblade, she dug into the ashes until she hit dirt, then dug a little more. Her hands were completely grey when she finished. She wiped her nose on her sleeve.

Placing the switchblade in the narrow divot in the earth,

Pinot covered it with dirt and ash. She held her hands over it for a long time.

"I'm so sorry," she said.

Drops fell on the mound of ashes and the backs of Pinot's hands. When she wiped the tears away with her palms, she could feel the gritty ash-dust left behind on her face.

Holding her hands in front of her, she pushed herself off her knees and went directly to Isak. "Show me your arms," she said.

Half-asleep, Isak held up his bare arms, the burns bright red. Pinot rubbed the last of her tears over them, flecked with ash.

***

It was a long way down to where the rocks made a way across the creek. Isak leaned heavily on Pinot's shoulder, her arm starting to cramp from supporting his back. The day was almost over, wisps of cloud glowing an ethereal pink through the trees.

They paused for a drink and to wash the ash from their faces. Fording the shallow water, they found the first red marker tied around a birch. Pinot stared at it as they passed, remembering her hunger-addled vision of Ed.

Twilight faded to darkness as they approached the cabin. "Around back," she whispered and Isak fell in step with her.

They carefully pushed their way through the overgrown trees along the rough side wall. Pinot leaned Isak against the cabin's side and continued around the corner as silent as a shadow. She opened the back door. It creaked and she paused, waiting for a response. Not hearing any, she snuck inside. She got one step into the kitchen when the bright beam of a flashlight hit her full in the face.

"Pinot!" a voice cried.

She felt a pressure around her back and shoulders. Blinking the brightness out of her eyes, she pulled away from the figure. It was Arissa.

"I thought you were a Grafter!" the older woman laughed.

"Oh," Pinot said, suddenly feeling self-conscious. Her last

interaction with Arissa had been antagonistic, at best. "Isak's outside. I'll bring him." She hurried out of the cabin and paused just outside the door. She took a few deep breaths of cool forest air, listening for animals in the brush. The night was silent. Rounding the corner of the cabin, she went to Isak.

"Is everything okay? I heard voices."

"It's Arissa," Pinot explained, supporting him as he limped towards the door. She didn't have the heart to tell him that she hadn't seen anyone else.

"Isak, thank goodness." Arissa welcomed him and helped him inside.

"You didn't hear us coming?" Pinot said, trying not to make it sound like a criticism.

"You're right, there should be someone standing watch out front, but we're worn out after—" She pursed her lips, then breathed deeply through her nose. "The past few days have been a lot for us to process. I thought I'd let them sleep." Arissa set the multi-purpose flashlight on the kitchen table, pulling up the plastic casing to convert it into a lamp.

Isak walked over to the sleeping residents scattered over the cabin's floor. Outside the circle of lamplight, he became a shadow.

"How many?" Pinot asked.

Arissa shook her head. "I don't know. I lost track of people. Some could've made it out without my knowing. I'm sure they'll come here once they feel safe enough. So far, it's just Ulway, Rhonda…May and Lucas…"

Pinot and Arissa stood in the kitchen, feeling the weight of the loss.

"But, we'll rebuild here," Arissa continued. "Start again as best we can. That's what I decided we would do if we ever lost the restaurant. You're surprised about that." Arissa smiled.

"I forgot how annoying your power is." Unhooking one of her backpack straps, Pinot unzipped the main pocket. She felt around in the darkness for the soft plastic bags and placed all of them on the kitchen table. "Here's some salve for Isak's burns. And if anyone else has injuries."

"We were lucky." Arissa placed a hand on Pinot's shoulder. "I had a lot of thinking to do after you left. You were right. I was being naive about our safety. But if we work together, I know we'll build something better this time around."

"I have to go," Pinot said.

"I know. You have other things you need to do." Arissa wrapped her in a deliberate hug. "And I'm proud of you for doing them."

"Heh," Pinot let out a breath and rested her chin on Arissa's shoulder, "like I need your approval."

"Thank you for taking care of Isak," Arissa said, letting her go. "You always have a home here, if you need it."

"Say goodbye for me." Stuffing her hands deep in her pockets, Pinot left the cabin without looking back.

Pinot almost made it to the creek before May caught up with her.

"Hey," May said, her long black hair flattened on one side, her coat buttons askew. "You're leaving?"

"Yeah," Pinot said, on guard.

"What about Isak? He's injured isn't he? You should stay until he's better."

"He should be fine with some rest and a good meal." Pinot relaxed. "Just don't let him scratch at the burns while they're healing."

They shared a knowing look—the memory of Pinot cutting the fingers off the gloves that were supposed to keep her from scratching at her burns all those years ago.

"I'm glad you and Lucas are okay," Pinot said, about to leave.

"Pinot." May hesitated. "I...treated you badly. You were just trying to help me, and I...I said things that hurt you. I did things that hurt you. I'm sorry. And I'm...sorry about what I did to Ed, about Jax. About everything." May brushed her palm over her eyes.

Pinot placed a hand on May's shoulder. "I'm sorry, too. I hope you'll find happiness here, May."

"You don't have to leave. I don't want you to."

The pressure of May's words hit Pinot in the chest. "I have to go." Pinot's voice wavered. "I'll be okay."

May sighed and the pressure on Pinot lifted. "Be careful." With a tight smile, May headed back up the path to the cabin.

Pinot crossed the creek. Moonlight filtered through the trees as she found her way to one of her old campsites. In the morning, she'd pick up Jax's tracks and follow them, wherever they went, however far they went. Even to the end of the world.

Chapter 14
Cabinhouse

The cabin was downright tiny when it had to sleep six.

Isak folded up his blanket and added it to the pile next to the couch. Rhonda was slowly running a broom across the floor where they'd slept packed next to each other—Arissa's feet next to the top of his head, Lucas in a small nest separating him and May. Ulway had slept on the couch the night before—they all took turns—and Rhonda curled up between Arissa and the front window. Nothing stopped them all from spreading out into the kitchen, but the closeness brought unspoken comfort for now. In the coming days, they'd have to figure out better sleeping arrangements.

Isak was the last one up. He went into the bathroom—the toilet long dry and a bucket of water in the counter-set sink. He found a clean face cloth among the others crammed together on the towel rack, wet it, and patted the healing burns on his arms and face with cool water. The flaking sections itched like mad, but he suppressed the idea of scratching, of wanting to scratch. He had to live with the healing—every itchy, burning, flaky moment of it.

He left the bathroom. The cabin was empty except for Ulway, who was sitting at the kitchen table duplicating cans of soup.

"Morning, Ulway!" Isak said, stopping by the table to take a handful of tiny crabapples from the fruit bowl. "How are you doing?"

Ulway smiled shyly, setting down the cans of soup. "I'm good. How are you?"

Isak didn't let the question settle too deep. "Good!" he said, signing at the same time. They'd all agreed to keep practising. To keep Catherine's knowledge alive.

His smile faltering, Ulway returned to duplicating soup cans. Isak didn't want to stare, but it was amazing to see what Ulway could do. Amazing to think that he'd been using it all along to keep them alive. "Thanks for doing that," Isak said, the phrase failing to sum up his feelings.

Ulway's wide face broke into a full smile. "You're welcome," he said, adding another soup can to the line across the table.

Biting into one of the sweet-sour apples, Isak continued through the kitchen and out the back door. Birdsong and sunlight drew him further onto the flattened wild grass that made up the cabin's yard.

Arissa was in the middle of plotting out a new garden. Four earthen cavities marked the corners of the soon-to-tilled square. The day before, they'd all taken turns digging out the bins of summer supplies he and May had buried there almost two years earlier.

May stood nearby as Lucas sifted through a little pile of leaves and dirt. She was wearing an old dress from one of the bins, brushstrokes of purple, red, brown, and blue across a plain white canvas. Her long dark hair was braided away from her pale forehead. There were bags under her eyes, but in spite of everything they'd been through in the days since the fire, she seemed happier.

Happier? That couldn't be the right word. But the heaviness in her shoulders, the distant stare, the small grimaces that had worried him at the restaurant the past few weeks were nowhere to be seen.

She noticed his presence across the yard, found his eyes with a questioning look, an openness.

He wanted to know where that burden had gone. He wanted to hear her voice, feel her close to him.

He let himself want it—

He was sitting down, the log bench solid underneath him. His hand pressed against the rough surface, scales of bark, patches of moss. The cool forest stirred in front of him, clearing away the faint smell of burnt wood.

"Has it been long?" he asked May, her dress-covered knee leaning against his.

"No. I thought you'd be here. Arissa's watching Lucas."

A breeze fluttered the leaves ahead of them. Isak knew that behind him were burned remnants, charcoal stumps. But their bench had survived. They'd survived. In the silence, with their knees touching, Isak was content.

"I'm sorry about Sophie," May said after a while. "I know how much she meant to you."

He didn't need May's ability to know that she was suffering the loss of the restaurant and their friends as much as he was. He tentatively reached an arm around her shoulders.

"Now what?" she said as they sat together, the ruins behind them, the forest ahead.

"I don't know," Isak replied. He waited in the unknowing, not wanting to be anywhere else.

Chapter 15
Pinot Meets an Old Friend

South of the forest, the wasteland was barren. Grey, flat, and lifeless. Pinot felt as if she had gone back in time to the first months after the Event.

A figure came toward Pinot across the desolation. Pinot stood up from studying the SU tracks, deciding to let the stranger come to her, readying herself for a fight.

The figure was lean, wearing runners, slacks, and a tweed blazer over a faded paisley button-up shirt. Their hands were at their sides, empty. As their face came into view, Pinot could make out brown skin, grey eyes behind round glasses, black hair pulled back from their forehead, revealing a single red dot.

They smiled softly as they reached her. "Pinot, it's Eliot."

"Eliot?" Pinot said, amazed. She remembered her, one of the scientists who lived in the SUs several years ago, part of Jax's unlikely gang. Pinot had considered Eliot a friend on the long way between Ed's convenience store and *Ulway*'s restaurant, but had never seen her outside of her bronze machine. "Did you know I was here?"

"I saw your heat signature on the SU's environmental scanner. But don't worry, I jammed Jax's sensors so he won't see you. Come with me."

Pinot followed Eliot as the wasteland horizon curved to reveal the cluster of two dozen bronze domes. Reaching the edge of the SUs, Eliot climbed up the side of one of them, opened the top hatch, and dropped inside. Pinot followed, closing the hatch after her.

Having never been inside a SU, Pinot was momentarily speechless. Hidden inside the bronze dome was a relatively normal room, featuring a fold-out bed, a kitchenette, and a treadmill. A wide padded chair was set at the front of the SU, facing a curved wall of screens monitoring the surroundings. Folded up into the ceiling were hydraulic arms and hardware that Pinot didn't recognize.

"Jax won't see or hear us in here," Eliot said. "I've set up a recording so it looks like I'm asleep." Eliot sat in the control chair and spun to face her.

Pinot settled onto the edge of the bed. "What's Jax doing out here?"

"Waiting for you, I think," Eliot replied seriously. "He destroyed the restaurant."

Pinot's hands clenched. "I know."

"I'm sorry that I couldn't stop it."

"Not your fault."

Eliot crossed her hands over her knee. "I have a lot to tell you," she sighed. "Would you like a drink?"

"Yes."

Eliot moved to the kitchenette and filled two cups with water from a spigot in the wall. "When we ran into you last month, I couldn't believe how much you'd grown up."

"Not like I was a kid when we met."

"You're right." Eliot measured spoonfuls of pink crystals from a jar and mixed them into the cups of water. "These days, it feels like I've lived way longer than I have."

"I always imagined you wearing glasses, you know. Smart scientist type."

"High praise." Eliot handed her a cup. "Lemonade." Taking her own, she settled back into the control chair. "Where do you want me to start?"

Pinot took a sip, the drink filling her mouth with a sweet-bitter taste. "The night we arrived at Arissa's restaurant."

Eliot took a deep draught of her lemonade. "I'll warn you, this story is not a happy one. But I want you to know what happened to me, to us, so you can understand what we need to do next."

Pinot nodded. "Whenever you're ready."

Eliot's Account Of The Survival Units, Jax, and the Destruction Of *Ulway's Restaurant and Retreat Centre*

I'll start with the night we originally found *Ulway's Restaurant and Retreat Centre*. We waited outside the restaurant, you remember. Everything was so unexpected: the forest, the log building with candles in the windows. Jax had gone inside with you and the rest of your friends. Even though it was the middle of the night, some of us got out of the SUs to take a closer look at the forest. Before reaching the edge of the woods that morning, we couldn't predict that such a large patch of natural Earth still existed. The biggest area we'd seen up until then was the acre of overgrown farmland where we buried Keats. We were grateful to you, you know. If you hadn't been there, I think Keats's death would've been too much for Jax.

Anyway, Jax came storming out of the restaurant. He didn't say anything, just made a circling motion with his hand. We packed back into our SUs and followed him down the hill, over a creek, out past the treeline to the wasteland. Guided by Matthew's navigational knowledge, we headed due west. We didn't see another soul for days. Jax barely slept or ate, just trudged ahead. We were worried about him. He didn't tell anyone what had happened, only that if we met you, May, Isak, or Ed again, we shouldn't trust you.

We reached Summerland, which was another big surprise. We'd heard about a settlement in the far west, but didn't expect one so large. Jax went into town for the night while we kept the SUs a fair distance away. He came back the next morning completely wiped but in a much better mood. He said a few of us could come back to town with him to pick up supplies. The greater town area was still being built then, but the courtyard was set up for trading. I was one of the three who braved the "outside" to go with him. We exchanged foodstuffs for some tools we were missing. Interacting with strangers outside of our SUs was something we hadn't experienced in a long time. It was exhilarating to match eyes with other people and wonder about their secret lives.

After a couple of days in Summerland, we rejoined our group and continued west. Jax became much more verbose, discussing how we would live safe from betrayers and manipulators, would start a colony of our own on the coast. He made it sound idyllic. I for one welcomed the idea. We'd been on the move ever since the Event—to have some time in one place would make for an excellent point of study. I was anxious to get readings from the Pacific, to see how the Event had affected the ocean ecosystems. It was hard, back then, to know what to expect.

All of us who were part of the original Survival Unit program always tried to gather as much data as we could, to see if we could make sense of what had happened to the world. The first couple of months after the Event, we gathered samples, traded hypotheses, moved over the land in search of answers. And when we ran into Jax, he promised to help us find those answers, in honour of his parents who had invented the SUs. But of course, you know all of that already.

We hit the west coast a few days later. We realised that the sand and rocks underneath us were actually part of the ocean floor. The water levels had receded a fair distance, well beyond usual low tide: somehow, the Event had removed or misplaced a vast area of the ocean.

We stopped a little ways away from the cliff ahead, which was really the ocean shelf that had been exposed. Jax walked right up to the edge and leaned over. Then something impossible happened. I'm still trying to get my head around it. Jax must've had a kind of power brought out by the Event. Like your power of healing, Pinot. When he turned back from the cliff, a huge wave crested over the cliff and rushed over our SUs. I remember climbing up to the hatch, trying to get out, but it was locked. The controls didn't respond. I was suddenly very tired. I barely made it to the bed before I blacked out. There was a thought right before I lost consciousness: the knowledge that Jax had done this and that I would never wake up again.

I didn't know it at the time, but Jax had put us into hibernation mode by overriding the controls in Matthew's SU and programming the rest of our SUs to move to life support when we reached the coast. Hibernation mode was an untested feature that had been included as an extreme last resort in case of radiation, famine, or other disasters that the world before the Event could conceive of. During hibernation, the SUs monitored our vitals and bodily needs through these silver rings we wear over our shoulders. The thin looping wires attach to the skin over our ribs, interacting with our systems through transmitters inside the wires. I was very lucky that I made it to the bed. Some of us spent the hibernation period on the floor or in the control chair, and woke up bruised and with muscular atrophy. We were in hibernation, off and on, for almost three years.

It was horrible. Every few months, Jax would wake us up and rave through the announcement system about how he was keeping us safe, that we had nothing to worry about, and that he would make the people who betrayed us pay. We'd have time to eat something solid, tend to our wounds, beg for him to let us go, before he'd hit the warning bell and throw us back into hibernation. At some point, Jax let slip that the SUs were underwater, and that really sealed the prospect of doom for most of us. I suppose he had kept one of the SUs above to control the hibernation cycles and to keep us in line. It was truly horrible, Pinot. I feel sick every time I think about those years in stasis, the sheer inhumanity of it. We knew then that Jax had gotten completely twisted and tried to find ways past his controls. But it was no good. There wasn't enough time between the hibernation periods to do much. And when Jax decided to cut our communications with each other—I can't even explain how hopeless it was.

Finally, I woke up to Jax's announcement that we would be leaving our colony for a mission. He'd found schematics in one of the old SUs that we left behind at Keats's grave—somehow, he'd gotten them back. The schematics were for a destructive weapon. While we were under, Jax had built it. The SUs were never meant to be weapons. But the project had been government-funded, and the potential for using the SUs as combat machines must've been on the radar from the beginning. I felt sick from my naivety and from the trauma my body had undergone for years without my consent.

The first place he destroyed was an old bottling factory. I was shocked to see that there were heat readings inside the building—people. I tried to get through to Jax's comm to convince him not to use the weapon, but he locked me out. He didn't trust any of us. Weeks of incinerating ruins up the coast followed. Then, Jax took us east.

It was no surprise that as soon as we reached Summerland, everyone left him. I'd worked on an override code for the hatches, not bothering to touch the auto-pilot or hibernation controls, since I thought Jax would have a tight grip on those systems. The hatch mechanism was a lot easier to hack, and I spent every waking moment on our way to Summerland working on it. As soon as we were in sight of the town, I released the hatches on all the SUs except for the one Jax was controlling. Everyone escaped. Except me.

"Ignore those ungrateful maggots," Jax videoed to me. It was the first time I'd seen him in years: he had grown into an angry, hateful man, no longer the teenager who had given us so much hope. "You and I have work to do."

He thought one of the others had instigated the hatch override. I'd routed it through multiple systems to make it look that way. Because I chose to stay. I had to. All of the data we'd collected after the Event was inside the SUs. I couldn't leave it. I promised myself that I would somehow take the SUs back from Jax, and stop him from doing anything harmful with them. I was outwardly supportive, all the while working on a way to disarm the weapon he had built. We moved on from Summerland, travelling in a pattern I didn't understand. Whenever we came across lone buildings in the wasteland, anything resembling a shelter or a structure, Jax destroyed them.

The weapon, I should mention, is explosive. It propels hydrogen taken from the atmosphere at a highly concentrated rate and ignites it. I won't go into further detail, but the effects of the weapon are extremely destructive. I believe that Jax was testing the weapon on those structures, fine-tuning it before getting to his actual target.

There was one building he destroyed that was different. It was a low concrete structure that looked like a prison. Jax got out of his SU to enjoy the effect of the weapon, ignoring the people rushing out of the building, some of them with guns. Jax incinerated them with the weapon, taking out half of the building in the process. There was a single heat reading, one person, who escaped out the back. The rest were swallowed up by flames.

Finally, Jax sent me the schematics for the weapon. He wanted to know if I could think of any way to further optimise the design. Although Jax had an exceptional talent for managing the SUs and their systems, I was the only real scientist left. I delayed, hummed and hawed, told him that science took time and if I made a mistake, the results could be disastrous.

But he lost patience. I was so invested in planning the best way to disarm or destroy the weapon that I didn't notice when we arrived at the restaurant. Jax kept our destination a secret, and I didn't expect him to attack again until the weapon was improved in some way. I heard the weapon go off, a huge boom that showed up on my SU's sensor. I turned on my viewscreen in time to see the restaurant in flames.

Chapter 16
Pinot and the End

Her story told, Eliot sat back in the control chair.

Pinot set her cup on the floor and took Eliot's thin hands in both of hers. "What can I do?"

Eliot squeezed her hands and let go. She turned the control chair to face the screens. Entering a command, Eliot brought up a blue map covered in white markers and dotted trails. A cluster of empty circles filled the middle of the screen. "This is us," she pointed at a circle on the edge of the cluster. "Jax is right in the middle." The circle in the centre blinked red. "I've figured out a way to disconnect the weapon, but I need to get to Jax's controls without him around. I can override his hatch lock from here, but I need someone to draw him out, distract him. I think that you're the only person he'd come out for." Eliot closed the screen and turned her chair to face Pinot. "Will you help me?"

"Eliot," Pinot said. "You're the most badass punk I've ever met."

"Well, it's all for science, isn't it?" she smiled wryly.

"I'm ready when you are."

Eliot climbed up and out of the SU. Pinot ditched her backpack by the control chair and took one last look around. It was truly incredible what people could build; equally as terrible was how it could be misused.

Pinot followed Eliot into the dim light of a cloudy day, and dropped down next to her on the benign dust of the deep wasteland.

"Are you sure he'll come out for me?" Pinot asked.

Eliot paused then nodded grimly. "You're the only one left for him to punish." Eliot buttoned up her brown tweed coat. "I'll need about half an hour to completely disarm the weapon."

"I'll give it everything I got." Pinot gripped Eliot's shoulder. Then, she headed towards the centre of the bronze circle, where Jax's SU waited.

Stopping a couple feet away, Pinot popped the collar of her leather jacket. She took her time putting on each fingerless glove. Gripping the pen lid in her left pocket, she sauntered up to Jax's SU. "Hey, you Opaldine piece of shit!" Pinot kicked the hard bronze exterior of the machine. "I wanna talk to you!"

After a moment, the hatch of the SU opened and Jax emerged. His hair was slicked back from his forehead, his cheeks sallow, his eyes gleaming with malice. He studied her with disgust. "So. No more names. About time." He spat into the air, the glob of saliva hitting the side of the SU and trailing down the smooth metal surface. "You wanna talk, Millerite? Let's talk."

Pinot started walking away, expecting him to clamber down after her. When he didn't, she turned back, furious. "Not from up there, you self-righteous prick!"

"You really think I'm going to lower myself to your level?"

Crossing her arms, Pinot smirked. "Outside of that machine, you're nothing!"

Jax's face shattered into a wide grin. He climbed halfway down the SU and jumped off, landing heavily on his feet. "You're going to regret saying that, Pinot, oh Pinot, you are…" He slowly moved towards her.

Pinot turned her back, knowing that Jax was in far too deep now to retreat. She kept ahead of his methodical pace, drawing him out to the edge of the hibernating domes, where he wouldn't see or hear Eliot get into his SU. She caught sight of the forest in the distance and faced him, as if the living set piece was the reason she'd brought him out here.

Jax stopped, mere metres away.

"How could you do that?" Pinot pointed back at the forest, at the remnants of the restaurant, exposing the infinity symbol on her wrist.

"Burn those fucking backstabbers to ash? It was my pleasure."

"And not just them," Pinot continued, the rage spilling over. "I saw other places, too. Places you burned down, people you killed. People I cared about! Why are you doing this?"

"Because they're all weak." Jax spread his hands as if the answer was obvious. "And because you deserve to be punished." His mouth twisted.

Pinot tensed, ready for an attack.

But Jax continued, beginning to circle around her. "I shouldn't have run away when I found out what your May-witch was doing to me. Changing my feelings, manipulating me like some puppet! I should have killed you all where you stood." His voice grew dangerous as he planted his feet, his back to the SUs. "I had a lot of time to think about how you made a fool out of me, Pinot. I thought you were different. I knew you were. But you didn't follow me. You stayed with them! You chose *them*! You didn't know what May and Ed were doing? Who cares! You didn't follow up, Millerite. You didn't try to make it right. You picked the easy way out, and I despise you for doing that!"

Pinot felt a trembling in her core, a gut punch that she hadn't expected. "You blame me, then." She couldn't keep the wavering out of her voice.

"Thought I still loved you?" Jax sneered. "Maybe I never really did." He calmly took a knife out of his pocket. "I'm going to kill you now."

Pinot froze, everything in her being tuned to the knife. Jax would kill her, she knew, and would enjoy doing it. Anything good in him had been drained away while he stewed in his hatred, for years, alone.

When he rushed her with the knife extended, her instincts

took over. Once again, she was the wild animal who hunted Grafters in the woods, she was the deranged doctor who had disembowelled a man for threatening her friends, she was the street-punk who got drunk off of violence and answered to no one. She grabbed Jax's wrist and wrenched the knife aside, head-butting his nose.

He swore, backing up to recover, blood gushing down over his lips, his chin. He stared at her; the blood stained his sharpened teeth.

He positioned himself to attack again, but she rushed him first, shouldering his midsection. Jax toppled backwards and lay on the bare earth, struggling to catch his breath.

Pinot reached over to pick him up by the collar, a fist overhead, but he kicked out her legs. She staggered to the ground a few feet away.

Breathing heavily, Pinot sat up, leaning back on her arms.

Jax groaned and slowly sat up to face her, matching her breathing, pinning her with his intense brown eyes.

They watched each other, wary. Jax didn't make a move. Pinot waited. Their breathing slowed and Jax's expression eased.

"Are you sure you want it this way, Pinot? Do you really want to kill the only person who understands you? Really understands?"

Pinot shook her head against him, remembering the ruins, the charred bodies. "You're not the person I knew before. You kill and destroy—"

"How is that different? Hmm?" Jax shuffled closer to her, so close she could smell him. Blood and salt and sweat. "How many people have you killed? One? Two? How many?"

She looked away.

"Yeah, I thought so. So accept it before you die: you deserve what I'm giving you." Jax swung his arm around and buried the knife into her thigh.

Shocked into silence, Pinot stared at the black metal handle growing from her leg.

She gripped it, tightened her hand, and wrenched it free.

"You'll have to try harder than that," she said through the pain.

Leaning forward, Pinot drove the knife into Jax's thigh. Blood welled around the wound and dripped onto the dust of the wasteland.

Jax started to laugh. "You see?" he managed. "We're the same." Gritting his reddened teeth, Jax slowly slid the knife out of his leg. His intense gaze reached into her. Blood shone on the blade.

Pinot scuffled backwards, but Jax was already on top of her, gripping her wrists with one hand, a knee digging into her sternum. The knife hovered overhead, dripping both of their blood onto her cheek.

"Farewell, farewell, farewell," Jax repeated wistfully. His red teeth clenched in a demented grin. He brought the knife down into Pinot's chest and twisted it.

Flesh tearing, ribs cracking, blood on his hands welling over the knife handle, running down the front of her leather jacket.

Jax pushed himself up, standing over Pinot's body. A feeling of elation took hold of him. Perhaps it was the effect of her blood, so much of it on his skin granting him her life energy. A sense of release from the past throbbed through him like a drug. As he limped away, Jax knew that from now on, he would be unstoppable. He would destroy the weak insects that crawled across the wasteland in the guise of human beings. He would burn it all to the ground.

A sound stopped him in his tracks. Boots scraping on dirt, a low moan in a voice he used to treasure more than anything else in the fucked-up godforsaken world. And as he turned in disbelief, he remembered with astounding clarity the way her mouth had tasted, the gleam of moonlight in her hair. She was close to him, their bodies matched in a way they would never be again.

And then, he felt nothing. His memory of her drifted into silence as his body fell to the earth, his own knife buried in his heart.

Pinot stumbled past him, pressing the open wound in her

chest. Blood trailed behind her. A few more steps, and she crumpled. She could smell the earth, feel it under her, cradling her as a good mother holds a sleeping child. Here, she could find peace. Rest. A place to call home at last. The end.

Chapter 17
Rhonda's Eulogy

They stood in a circle around a single white flower that had already pushed up through the ashes of the restaurant. Arissa, Ulway, May holding Lucas, Isak, and Rhonda—the survivors.

It was Rhonda's turn to say something.

She studied the grey-black surface between her runners. *It wasn't fair!* The mantra that had rung through her for the past week swelled. The fire, the death. But slowly, a harmony had grown up around it. *This was part of how it must be.* Not how it had happened. Not the destruction. Not the disease. Not the Event. But how it must be overall. Death, part of life, and vice versa. Humans were not above that. Life, death, rebirth. Cycles older than the earth.

She was standing on that earth, part of it—somehow, still alive.

"Um," she said, her uncertain beginning loud in the ruins. "You've already said…" Rhonda swallowed back the sob in her chest that had not let up for days, sitting under her ribs like a bubble of air under a river rock. "You've already said so much about the restaurant, and everyone…"

She suddenly clicked into the moment—smelt the charred wood, felt the light breeze on her face, saw Arissa's encouraging nod.

"It's hard to be back here," Rhonda said, her voice carrying above the wind. "It's very hard. I can't be here without thinking about Nick."

The sob was there again, threatening to burst. She breathed through it, adjusting Milo's watch that sat snugly around her left wrist. "You know, when Milo and I lived at the school, before we came here, I thought that our lives were complete. We didn't need anybody else. But I was wrong, wasn't I?"

May gave her a tight smile from across the circle, Isak nodding slowly as Lucas reached over and lazily grabbed a bit of his hair. Ulway, the tallest of them, stared at the flower, his aunt resting a hand on his shoulder.

Rhonda took another breath, following Ulway's lead—she delivered the next words to the small flower in the centre of their circle. "This isn't the first ending we've faced. It won't be the last. All we can do is take what we've learned and make another start. That's how we honour our friends, alive or passed on. I hope that they are still part of the land around us. That their end was a new start as well. That they'll help us with our way forward. We're not alone."

And saying the words, with her friends around her, Rhonda knew that they were true.

Chapter 18
Pinot After Death

The darkness passed and Pinot found herself somewhere bright and soft. Was there something after death, after all?

A hand gripped hers and she focused on the steady touch, letting it pull her back into the world. But the world was painful, and she gripped the hand in hers and arched her back against it.

"It's alright," a voice cut through the pain. "Take a breath. Relax. That's it."

The world came into focus. A ceiling. A light blue curtain around the bed she lay on. Someone near her, a hand in hers. Tweed.

"Eliot?" she managed, lifting her head from the pillow. The movement stabbed needles through her chest and she fell back, focusing on her breath until the pain receded.

"You're alive," Eliot smiled from the chair next to her bed.

"Where are we now?"

"Summerland. This is the clinic. I think you know it."

"And Jax?"

Eliot placed her other hand over Pinot's. "He's dead."

"Yes," Pinot said, a different kind of pain filling her chest. "I thought he was."

"I should let you rest," Eliot said.

"No, it's okay." Pinot took a deep breath, wincing a little as her lungs pressed against the wound. "Can you tell me what happened?"

Eliot lifted a hand to readjust her glasses. "After you left, I got into Jax's SU and was able to disarm the weapon. There was an eject setting encoded in the program, in case the weapon ever jammed or malfunctioned. I deleted all the schematics and information about the weapon from the computer. Then I went to find you."

"And I was pretty much dead."

"I got you into an SU and hooked you up to the life support system. It had to restart your heart once, but after that and a lot of bandaging, your body's healing abilities took over. It was enough to minimise the blood loss and give the SU time to provide support for your other vitals. The med says you'll have a scar on your heart muscle, but apart from that, you should be okay."

"You saved my life." Pinot gripped her hand. "Thank you. And don't say it was just for science," she finished with a weak laugh.

Eliot smiled. "I won't."

"Well, she's awake is she?" Clem leaned into Pinot's field of vision. "And pretending the pain isn't that bad, am I right? Fayette!" They waved a hand and another med appeared. "Fayette's going to make sure you drink your herbal tea."

"Not you too," Pinot groaned, recognizing Fayette's short golden hair. "Is this really how you run this place, Clem? You nurse people back to health and then expect them to work with you?"

"Exactly!" Clem beamed at Pinot. "I can't wait until you're well enough, there's so much research we have to do! Vaccines to make, medicines to refine! And with the astounding life support technology in Eliot's machines to work with, there's nothing we can't accomplish! We'll be so busy you won't have time to go on these dangerous escapades across the wasteland anymore!"

Eliot stifled a laugh as Fayette rolled her eyes.

Pinot, under the influence of her near-death experience, or

something else entirely, fully saw them for the first time, each and together in the ring they made around her: Fayette's golden hair contrasting the worn medical apron tied over her about-to-burst pregnant belly; Eliot's eternal tweed blazer and thoughtful eyes behind her round glasses; Clem's wild brown and grey hair and exasperating cheerfulness.

"So?" Clem asked as they held out their wide, open hand. "What do you think?"

"What the hell," Pinot said, taking Clem's offered hand in her own. "I'll stick around."

Epilogue

WELCOME TO THE CABINHOUSE ARCHIVE

FADE TO:

[*A woman sits in a faded armchair. In her thirties, she is broad-shouldered, tall, and heavy-set with medium brown skin; her eyes are deep brown and her hair is long and black, draped like two curtains over her black t-shirt. Her jeans are patched but well taken care of. On her wrist is an old silver watch. She smiles slightly, then places her hands on her knees.*]

WOMAN: Hello. I'm Rhonda, as you probably know, and this is the archive. What started out as a cardboard box in a closet now has its own room in the main building that we like to call the Hub. The archive is split into three sections: Pre-Event Materials, which you'll find back there—[*Rhonda lifts a hand to indicate the wall behind her, lined with two large shelving units packed with books, boxes, and binders.*]

[*Her hand returns to her knee as she nods to the left.*] You'll find research about the Event and archival copies of Summerland's Survival Unit data in the low cabinet by the window. And on the shelf next to me, the history of our settlement and the people we've lost along the way.

[*She readjusts her watch, then crosses her hands in her lap.*]

There should be a binder next to this screen, with further instructions of where to find materials and how to handle them. We ask that you keep all materials inside this room, and keep all food and beverage outside of it. That means you, Lucas!

[*She playfully shakes a finger at the screen. Moving a hand to the armrest, she relaxes into a more serious tone.*]

Now, as part of the introduction to our archive, I also want to tell you why I'm making this video. For many of us, Jax's path of destruction was the first historical event of note after the Event itself. It's been ten years since we lost *Ulway's Restaurant and Retreat Centre*. Many of the physical records we had saved up to that point were lost.

After relocating here, I spent years restoring the archive: I remembered everything that I could, adding my own knowledge and many of your stories to the collection. Our trading relationships with Summerland and other havens contributed materials that were found or made on the wasteland, including a comprehensive copy of poems by ECB.

When we finally got a working computer again, I was able to download the copies of the original archive I had saved on a USB that escaped with me during the fire. After many years of work, I'm happy to say that all of the records have been restored, and then some!

[*She smiles and sits up in the chair.*]

I've also been fortunate to interview a lot of people about the loss of *Ulway*'s and the early days of our current settlement, Cabinhouse. In the past decade, Cabinhouse has grown to become a permanent trading site for the Western Wastes, and that's thanks to all of you. And it's important to know, I think, how that all came about. So make sure you check out the central display, which includes some eyewitness accounts and a timeline of the events leading up to the fire and the move to Cabinhouse. I hope you'll find it interesting.

[*Rhonda sees someone off camera and nods slightly, her smile tender.*]

Alright, that's all I got. If you have any questions, you know where to find me. Enjoy the archive, and keep taking care of each other out there.

THE END

Acknowledgements

When I started writing *The Patch Project* over a decade ago, I never dreamed that it would lead to a three book series. I have so many people to thank for their help, support, and encouragement while I worked on this book, and the series as a whole!

First of all, thank you to Adventure Worlds Press for making this series a reality! I absolutely love working on book projects with you and am always grateful for your collective know-how and kindness. Writing Wrecking Crew forever!

Thank you to all of the first readers for this book—Elizabeth J. M. Walker, Alexander Zelenyj, Hanan Hazime, Lydia Friesen, Ben Van Dongen, and Christian Laforet. Your insightful notes made me go into detail about the important stuff!

My incredible editor and friend Amilcar John Nogueira delayed the final draft of this book by giving the most in-depth structural edits I've ever had to make. The book is much better thanks to their story-forging knowledge and their kind listening.

I also want to thank Elly Blake, Nico VC, Jasper Appler, Joanna Kimmerly-Smith, Cecilia Miller, Zach Supina, Sarah Kivell, Owen Swain, Matt Caron, Caroline Lehrer, Tasha Donnelly, Karl Parakenings, Sean Marzec, Sara Rolfes, Dawn Supina, Shelly Campbell, and Michelle Heumann for always being willing to chat about the creative process.

A special shout out to my fantastic family and friends for your support and encouragement. All the times you offered meals, a place to stay, a video call, a letter, a message—all are so appreciated!

And as always, Peter gets the final line. This year of change and starting over has been difficult, but there's no one I'd rather be sitting next to, on a bench with coffee in the woods, than you.

Brittni Brinn (she/her) writes science fiction from a tower and sometimes a cottage in Nova Scotia, Canada. She has a Master's in Creative Writing from the University of Windsor. Her favorite things include books from friends, exceptional cups of coffee, and rocks kicked up by the ocean.

Website: brittniinink.wordpress.com
Facebook: brittniinink
Instagram: brittni_in_ink

AdventureWorldsPress.com